A TIME TO CARE

A CHRISTIAN ROMANCE

JULIETTE DUNCAN

A TIME FOR EVERYTHING SERIES - BOOK 2

Cover Design by http://www.StunningBookCovers.com

Copyright © 2019 Juliette Duncan

All rights reserved.

FOREWORD

HELLO! Thank you for choosing to read this book - I hope you enjoy it! Please note that this story is told from two different points of view – Wendy, an Australian, and Bruce, a cowboy from Texas. Australian spelling and terminology have been used when in Wendy's point of view – they're not typos!

As a thank you for reading this book, I'd like to offer you a FREE GIFT. That's right - my FREE novella, "Hank and Sarah - A Love Story" is available exclusively to my newsletter subscribers. Go to http://www.julietteduncan.com/subscribe to get the ebook for FREE, and to be notified of future releases.

I hope you enjoy both books! Have a wonderful day!

Juliette

PROLOGUE

"There is a time for everything,
and a season for every activity under the heavens:
a time to be born and a time to die,
a time to plant and a time to uproot,
a time to kill and a time to heal,
a time to tear down and a time to build,
a time to weep and a time to laugh,
a time to mourn and a time to dance,
a time to scatter stones and a time to gather them,
a time to embrace and a time to refrain from embracing,
a time to search and a time to give up,
a time to keep and a time to throw away,
a time to tear and a time to mend,
a time to be silent and a time to speak,
a time to love and a time to hate,
a time for war and a time for peace."
Ecclesiastes 3:1-8

CHAPTER 1

*S*ydney, Australia

She shouldn't be here. Paige Miller knew that the moment she walked into the nondescript clinic in downtown Kings Cross. But the fact remained, she didn't want this baby. The thought of aborting it abhorred her, but she had no option. Ignoring the voice inside her head, she made herself known to the girl behind the desk, took a seat and waited.

Sitting rigidly, her heart thudded in her ears while the overhead fan wobbled and stirred warm air around the small room. Pro-abortion posters covered the walls. *My body, My choice, My rights. Abortion, never an easy choice, sometimes the best choice, always a woman's choice. Everyone deserves the right to their own choice.* Paige bit her lip. She had no choice. Abortion was her only option.

Moments later, a middle-aged woman wearing a smart suit and heels opened the consulting room door and waved her in.

Standing, Paige walked the few steps to the room and sat

on the chair the woman indicated. She introduced herself as Marcia McClelland. Her voice was educated but not pompous. Her hair, a rich, glowing auburn, was pulled back in a low bun. Peering over her designer glasses at Paige, she was not what Paige had expected to see at the free clinic one of her Goth friends had told her about.

"We support a woman's right to choose what happens with her own body," the woman said, her voice softening, "but you have to be completely comfortable with the decision to abort your baby before we'll proceed." Leaning back in her swivel chair, she removed her glasses and twiddled them between her fingers. "We always wait a week between the first consultation and the procedure to allow time for reflection. It's never an easy decision, and no one can tell you what's best for you." She paused, placed her glasses on the table and steepled her fingers on the desk. "Do you have any questions?"

Paige lowered her gaze to her hands folded neatly in her lap. Unlike Marcia McClelland's perfectly manicured and polished nails, hers were chewed and ugly. They hadn't always been that way. Before she'd taken to living rough, she used to take care of herself, but now, without money, job or home, caring for her nails was not a priority.

Did she have any questions? Not really. She already knew that the foetus, *her baby*, had a heartbeat. That at thirteen weeks, it was almost eight centimetres long, fingerprints were forming on its tiny fingertips, and it weighed nearly thirty grams. And it had a soul. If she proceeded with the abortion, she'd be committing murder. The pro-abortionists either didn't believe that or didn't care, but, raised in a home where

Christian beliefs were taught and upheld, she did, even though she'd rather not.

She lifted her gaze. "No, I don't."

"Okay. Go home and think about it. Let us know by next Thursday if you wish to proceed, and if you do, we'll see you on Friday at 9 a.m. You'll be here for the day, but if all goes well, you'll be able to go home. Is there someone who can collect you late in the afternoon?"

Paige shrugged. "I'll find someone."

"Good. If you have any questions before then, please come in and ask. Or even if you just want someone to talk to. We know how emotionally stressful this time can be." The woman spoke with care and understanding. She'd probably had an abortion at some time herself, or why else would she be doing this job?

"Okay. Thank you." Paige's voice faltered. Standing, she offered the woman a small smile and shook her hand when it was offered. She couldn't wait to get out of there.

Stepping onto the footpath a few moments later, a heavy invisible weight crushed her shoulders. She desperately wanted to be rid of the baby, but she couldn't do it. As much as she didn't want it, she couldn't murder it. But how could she keep it? She could barely look after herself, let alone a baby.

Tears built behind her eyes. She'd made such a mess of her life. If only Dad had lived, everything would have been different. She wouldn't have dropped out of University, she wouldn't have hung out with Goths, she wouldn't have taken drugs, and she wouldn't be pregnant. It was God's fault. He could have saved Dad. But blaming God didn't solve her problem now. And He wouldn't help her. Why would He?

She needed to figure this out on her own. Her mantra since Dad died was that no one was looking out for her. Not even Mum, especially now she'd married her cowboy. So, she had to look out for herself. Life was what she made it. God didn't care about her. No one did. Sighing heavily, she crossed the busy road and headed back to the boarding house where she was living at Kings Cross. As she climbed the stairs to the third floor, the stench of stale urine, cigarette smoke and alcohol made her gag. She raced for the shared bathroom, dropped to her knees and vomited into the putrid toilet bowl. Collapsing onto the cold, dirty floor, despair descended on her and she sobbed uncontrollably. It wasn't fair. None of it was fair.

She couldn't live like this anymore. As much as she hated to admit it, she missed Mum's beautiful home on the harbour. How could she continue living in a dive like this when she could eat humble pie and go home? Mum would be shocked. Disappointed. But she'd look after her. With no money and no job, she really had no choice.

But she'd give it one more day. Maybe she could think of something better.

CHAPTER 2

*D*eciding to sell her family home was never going to be easy. Happy memories filled every wall and corner of the home where Wendy McCarthy and her first husband, Greg, had raised their three children, but the time had come. Now married to Bruce McCarthy, the Texan cowboy she'd met in Dublin a year earlier when he accidentally spilled coffee over her, she wanted to make new memories with him, and while they could make them there, in the harbourside home she loved so much, she knew he'd feel more comfortable in the country where there was space to keep horses and possibly even some cattle. It wouldn't compare with Cedar Springs, his family ranch in Texas that his eldest son Nate, and daughter-in-law, Alyssa, were now managing, but Wendy had been doing her research and knew there were ten-acre hobby farms on the north-western outskirts of Sydney she hoped he'd be happy with.

Leaning against the kitchen counter while waiting for the

kettle to boil, she gazed out the window at the harbour below. The view was spectacular. The water, smooth and deep blue, shimmered in the early morning sun. She'd never tire of that view. In fact, it was the reason she and Greg had decided to buy the house after returning from a year living and working in London as newlyweds. They'd both fallen in love with it, and since it was so close to the city and to their places of employment, they bought it without a second thought.

She'd thought they'd live their entire lives there, but God had other plans. Greg had died of a heart attack five years earlier, and although she'd had no plans to fall in love again and re-marry, she and Bruce both believed their chance meeting in Dublin was God-ordained. From the very first they were drawn to each other, and even now, recalling the three weeks they'd shared together in Dublin, London, Paris, and Venice made her heart flutter.

Silver-haired Bruce McCarthy had a certain magnetism she'd been powerless to fight. And truth be told, she didn't want to. Having lived on her own for four years, Wendy thanked God every day for giving her a second chance at love. It had been so unexpected but so special. They were kindred spirits. As a widower himself, Bruce knew exactly how she felt. He knew the challenges of adapting to life after losing a beloved spouse. How long the nights were, and how the days rolled together so that all sense of time was lost.

Bruce's first wife, Faith, had died in a car accident over ten years before, but he'd never dated another woman. Until Wendy. From their very first meeting there was a tangible bond between them, and their romance progressed quickly. He proposed in Paris. She hadn't agreed immediately, wanting to pray about it to ensure it wasn't just a holiday romance, but when he returned to Texas and she to Sydney, it didn't take long for her to know that the love they shared was real, and she accepted his proposal when he travelled to Sydney to attend her eldest daughter's wedding.

The kettle whistled, drawing her back to the present. She poured the boiling water into two mugs and waited for the tea bags to brew. Bruce hadn't pressured her in any way to sell the house. He said he was happy there. He filled the days when she was lecturing at University by doing some much-needed maintenance around the house, but she sensed it was hard for him knowing that she'd shared the house with Greg for more than thirty years. No doubt it would be similar for her when they visited his ranch. Bruce and Faith had lived there for many years, but since she and Bruce didn't plan to live there, Wendy knew she'd handle visiting just fine.

She was so thankful they could talk about their feelings for their previous spouses. Accepting that Greg and Faith would always hold a special place in their hearts, there was no need to pretend they'd never existed. But the time had come to move on. Wendy could hardly wait to see the expression on Bruce's face when she told him, although she dreaded to see Paige's.

Paige, her youngest daughter, still held God accountable for her father's death. She'd recently dropped out of University and moved out of the house. Wendy's heart ached for her lost daughter. Every day she committed her to the Lord and asked Him to move in her heart and to help her let go of her anger and disappointment towards Him. They all missed Greg, and no one knew why he'd been taken so young, but Wendy knew that Greg wouldn't want Paige to be blaming God. Growing up, they'd taught their children that God was a good God who loved them with His whole being, but being a Christian didn't shield them from suffering and pain. Having Jesus in their heart, did, however, give them strength to survive and endure, no matter what happened. Wendy prayed daily that Paige would remember those truths and return to the faith of her childhood one day soon. Before her life fully imploded.

She squeezed the teabags and tossed them into the bin, poured a small amount of milk into each, and then stirred a teaspoon of sugar into Bruce's. She'd tried to get him to cut sugar altogether, but he didn't seem able to give up that last teaspoon. She smiled to herself. At least he'd reduced it from the three he'd taken when they first met. Leaving her cup on the counter, she carried his up the stairs and along the hallway to their bedroom. Soft snores greeted her and she was tempted to let him sleep, but she had plans for today, and it was already after seven. Tip-toeing to his side of the bed, she set his cup quietly on the bedside table and paused to study the man who had so quickly captured her heart. His silver hair was receding and thinning, and his face, which had been tanned from many years in the Texan sun when they first met, had paled a little since living in the city, but his profile was still strong and she truly didn't care whether he was tanned or not.

His crystal blue eyes fluttered and opened and he gave her a smile that sent her heart racing. He had a way of making her feel like a giddy teenager, not a woman in her late fifties.

Wriggling to a sitting position, he adjusted the pillows behind his back, reached for her hand and pulled her gently towards him. "What are you doin' up so early, my darlin'?

Come back to bed." She'd never tire of his smooth Texan drawl.

She chuckled and resisted. "I'd love to, but you need to get up. I've got something planned for us today."

He angled his head. "Something that can't wait?"

"Yes." She sat on the bed beside him and stroked his hand. She'd prayed about moving and had finally felt it was the right time, but now, sitting here with Bruce, doubt suddenly clouded her mind. What if it wasn't the right thing to do? What if moving pushed Paige further away? Maybe she should pray about it again before saying anything. She let out a small sigh. But was there any harm in looking? They could talk to her three children before making any firm decisions.

Natalie, the eldest, and recently married to Adam, would be sad but would understand. Simon hadn't even bothered to collect his belongings that had been stored in the garage for years, and Wendy doubted he'd care where she lived. He seemed so distant, but she didn't know why. It was just Paige. Could she risk alienating her further when she seemed so lost already? But then, should she and Bruce put their plans and dreams on hold on the off-chance that staying in the house where Paige had been raised would help her face her issues? No. Perhaps moving to a new place, a new area, could be just the trigger that might cause Paige to let go of her anger and bitterness.

She met Bruce's gaze and swallowed hard. "I thought we might take a drive."

"Do you have somewhere in mind?" He cocked a brow as he drew circles on her hand with his finger.

She nodded. "The Hills District?"

He stopped circling and straightened, his eyes widening. "Where the hobby farms are?"

She smiled. "Yes."

"Does that mean what I think it does?"

Wendy couldn't help the grin that spread across her face. "Yes, it does. I'm finally ready to move."

"Oh, my darling. Are you sure? It's such a huge thing."

"Yes. I want a place we can truly call our own. There are too many memories here. Good ones, but they're not ours. I want us to build our own. And I know how much you'd like to have more space."

"What will the kids say?"

Wendy shrugged. "They'll be fine."

"Well, I have to say that's the best surprise. Not that I don't like this house. It's a lovely home, and I love being so near the harbour, but..."

Wendy lifted her finger to his lips. "I know. Let's go house hunting."

Half an hour later, after dressing quickly and downing their cups of tea and a piece of toast each, they left the harbourside suburb of Cremorne and headed west to where box-sized suburban blocks gave way to winding, leafy roads and hobby farms on properties that could fit several suburban streets inside them. It wasn't Texas, but Wendy hoped Bruce would feel more at home here than in the high-density inner-city suburb of Cremorne, as nice as it was. She knew he'd been looking at properties on the internet, and so had she, without him knowing. The question was, would they find a property they both liked?

"Why don't we grab some brunch and then look at some

places," she said as they approached a small stretch of boutique shops, art galleries and trendy cafés. One of the side streets had been closed off for the Saturday markets and bustled with people of all ages and descriptions, as well as dogs on leads, some large, some small, and even some designer ones that made Wendy laugh. Street musicians wearing hippy-styled clothing played music on a variety of instruments.

Bruce turned and gave her a smile. "Sounds perfect."

"It's a lovely area, isn't it?"

"It is." He parked the car under the shade of a blossom tree. In full flower, the sweet perfume tickled her nose and made her smile. He took her hand and they strolled along the pretty street, stopping to look at menus at the various cafés. They decided on the 'Wheel and Barrow', a rustic looking café that enticed them with the aroma of freshly baked bread and brewed coffee.

It seemed popular. Only one table was available inside, so they headed outside into an alfresco area under the shade of a large acacia tree. Water tumbling over polished stones created a relaxing and cooling atmosphere. Although busy, several tables were empty.

"Where would you like to sit, my darling?" Bruce placed his hand against the small of her back.

"I don't mind. You choose." She smiled at him.

"How about over there, beside the wheelbarrow." Colourful annuals filled a rustic wheelbarrow and trailed lazily over the side.

Wendy nodded. "Perfect."

He pulled a chair out for her. She sat and ran her left hand through the lavender in the pots on the stone wall beside the table. Lifting her palm to her nose, she inhaled the distinctive perfume and sighed nostalgically at the memories it invoked. She and Greg had planted a whole row of lavender along their driveway soon after they moved into the house at Cremorne. The lavender had since been replaced with a low growing nondescript hedge she wasn't terribly fond of, but when the children came along and they were both working, they'd had little time for gardening, and low maintenance became the mantra they lived by. She still kept a pot of the perfumed plant on their back deck, however.

Bruce sat opposite, and a waitress delivered menus, promising to return to take their orders.

"It seems the place to be," he said, glancing around at the tables which were now all taken.

"It certainly does. Their food must be good." Wendy picked up her menu.

They spent a few minutes making their choices, then placed their orders when the waitress returned as promised. After she left, Bruce took Wendy's hand. "Are you sure about this, Wendy? We'll need to find a new church, new friends, new everything, and it'll be a long commute to work for you."

She grinned. "That was another of my surprises. I've decided to quit work."

"No!"

She nodded. "I've been thinking ever since we got married that I should give it up, but I wasn't ready. Until now. I was reading my Bible yesterday and all of a sudden I had a sense that it was time to let go of things from the past and move onto whatever God has in store for us. So, yes, it would be a long commute to work, but no, I won't need to do it."

He studied her in earnest. "I don't know what to say, darlin'. That's a huge decision."

"I know." She gulped and looked down at their hands. It *was* a huge decision. Teaching and lecturing had been so much a part of her life for so long, and she'd miss it for sure, but God had other things in store for them. She just didn't know what. She lifted her gaze and met his. "It will mean we can spend all our time together. I won't have to leave you alone anymore."

His mouth twisted in a smile. "I like the sound of that! I do miss you when you're not home." As their gazes held, a tingle ran through her body. It still amazed her that she could feel this way. "And I miss you when I'm at work. It'll be wonderful to be with you all the time."

Their meals arrived. Crispy bacon and eggs on sourdough for him, Eggs Benedict with salmon for her, and two cappuccinos in mugs.

"Shall we give thanks?" he asked after the waitress left.

Smiling, she nodded and took his extended hand before bowing her head.

"Lord God, thank You for this food before us, but more than that, we thank You for Your abundant provision in every aspect of our lives, which we commit anew to You now. In Jesus' precious name. Amen."

"Amen," Wendy repeated softly after him. She so loved Bruce's way of giving thanks. It didn't matter where they were, he never failed to thank the Lord for His goodness. She was so blessed to have him as her husband.

They began to eat. Wendy had been right; the food was delicious. The sauce was to die for, the eggs were cooked perfectly, and the salmon, fresh and tasty. "This is wonderful. I think it's going to become my favourite place for breakfast," she said, setting her knife and fork neatly across the plate after mopping up the last bit of sauce with her toast.

"I agree," he said, "but there's too much. I don't think I can finish it." He toyed with a piece of crispy bacon but then set it down.

"That's not like you not to finish a meal, darling. Are you feeling all right?" Warning spasms of alarm erupted within her. Having beaten bowel cancer several years earlier, every time Bruce was slightly off colour, she immediately suspected its return even though he assured her often that he'd been given a clean bill of health.

"Yes, I'm fine. No need to worry. It was just a huge serving."

She pursed her lips. There was no use arguing with him, but she'd seen him eat twice that amount for breakfast. "As long as you're okay."

"I am." He spoke quietly and his eyes held a look that brooked no argument. "Shall we venture forth and check out some of those properties now?"

"Yes. Let's go."

CHAPTER 3

*P*aige slumped onto the couch in her mother's house and stared at the ceiling, her heart heavy. If only she could have gone through with the abortion. Now she was stuck with an unwanted pregnancy.

She swiped at her eyes. She'd made a mess of everything, ruined her life. Last night she'd been tempted to take some pills and never wake up, but something had stopped her, just like something had stopped her from having the abortion. Mum would say it was God, but she and God weren't on talking terms since He'd ignored her plea to save Dad from dying. He could easily have saved him, but He obviously didn't want to. *What kind of God would do that?* Not one she wanted anything to do with.

She truly didn't want this baby. No way was she ready to be a mother, especially on her own. The father could be any number of men she'd dallied with since Colin Daley, a fellow Goth she'd thought for a while might have loved her, but ended their relationship, telling her he'd found someone else. She wouldn't want any of the others involved in her baby's life.

A heavy, invisible weight crushed her heart and her sobs intensified.

Some time later, her stomach rumbled and she remembered she hadn't eaten properly for days. Swinging her legs off the couch, her gaze was drawn to the photo on the wall. Her family. Mum, Dad, Natalie, Simon, and her, taken during a family vacation at the beach not long before Dad died. Life had been so simple then. It wasn't fair—Dad should still be alive. Blowing out a big breath, she headed to the kitchen.

WENDY TURNED the key in the door and sniffed. *Toast?* She frowned and turned to Bruce. "Do you smell something?"

He shrugged. "No."

Wendy stepped inside. Definitely toast. She walked down the hallway and peered into the kitchen. "Paige! It's so good to see you!" She stepped forward and held her arms out.

Paige lifted her chin and her eyes flooded with tears.

Wendy quickly closed the gap between them and drew her into her arms. "What's the matter, sweetheart?"

Paige began sobbing uncontrollably against her shoulder.

Holding her tight, Wendy kissed the top of her hair and prayed silently as pain for her daughter squeezed her heart. *Lord, bless my little girl. I don't know what's brought her home, but I thank You that she's here. Give me wisdom to know what to say and do.*

Over Paige's shoulder, Wendy caught Bruce's gaze. He gestured that he'd go upstairs. She nodded her appreciation.

Wendy tugged some tissues from the box on the kitchen counter and handed them to Paige. Taking them, Paige blew her nose and her sobs slowly eased. Wendy rubbed her back. Paige looked less than great. Her once lovely, shiny hair was dull and matted, and the body odour emanating from her suggested she hadn't washed in days, possibly weeks. But at least she'd come home. "Come and sit down, darling." She guided Paige to the couch in the sunroom and sat beside her. Wendy traced the tips of her fingers around her hairline. "It's okay, darling. Whatever's the matter, we can work through it together."

Wendy waited. Paige sniffed, keeping her gaze firmly fixed on her hands.

Her nails were chewed so low that dried blood stained the quicks. Wendy pushed back tears of her own. What had happened to her beautiful daughter? Pulling Paige to her chest, she closed her eyes and rocked her gently, like she used to do when Paige came home from school in tears after being teased by the boys down the street. "I love you, sweetheart. We'll take care of you. There's no hurry to tell me what's wrong."

Wendy lost track of how long they sat like that. Memories from long ago surfaced and flashed through her mind. She and Greg had been so excited to welcome their beautiful new daughter into the world. Paige had brought them such joy from the moment she was born with her sunny nature and enthusiasm for life. She remembered how excited they were when she took her first steps, and how she couldn't wait to start school. And how her testimony at her baptism when she was twelve had brought tears to their eyes. But then Wendy recalled Paige's sullen face at Greg's funeral. She couldn't accept that he was gone. That God hadn't answered their prayers when she'd prayed with such faith. They all had, but Paige hadn't accepted that sometimes God had other plans and we don't always get what we ask for.

But there'd been a glimmer of hope. Wendy recalled with fondness Paige's laughter as she sailed a small catamaran with Bruce's youngest son, Aiden, at their wedding in Fiji just six months earlier. There was hope. There was always hope.

"Would you like a cup of tea?" Wendy asked quietly.

Paige drew back, and blowing her nose, nodded.

Wendy smiled and then stood. "I'll be right back."

"Thank you." Paige's voice was barely audible, but at least she'd spoken.

While Wendy waited for the kettle to boil, she stared out at the harbour. A southerly wind had picked up, and the boats moored out front bobbed in the choppy water. But their anchors held. An old hymn came to mind, and Wendy prayed that Paige's anchor would also hold as she faced this storm in her life, whatever it might be. But Paige had shunned that anchor for almost five years. Would she now see her need for the Saviour who could provide strength for all of life's storms? Wendy prayed she would.

The kettle boiled and she proceeded to fill two mugs with the steaming water. She added an extra spoon of sugar to Paige's tea and placed several Anzac cookies on a small plate before placing the mugs and the plate on a tray which she carried to the sitting room.

Paige had barely moved, and her downcast demeanour tore

at Wendy's heart. Setting the tray on a small side table, Wendy eased herself onto the couch and offered a mug to Paige. "Here sweetheart. This will help."

Paige lifted her gaze and took the mug. "Thank you." Wrapping her hands around it, she held it to her lips and took small sips.

"Have a cookie." Wendy lifted the plate and offered it to her. Paige set her mug on the table and took one of the store-bought biscuits. She nibbled at it, which surprised Wendy. Paige was so thin, she'd expected her to gobble it down and ask for another.

The telephone rang but Wendy ignored it. Bruce answered it. His voice drifted down from upstairs, but she couldn't discern what he was saying. Wendy guessed it might be her eldest daughter, Natalie, since she often called in the late afternoon.

Wendy sipped her tea. She didn't want to push Paige, but she'd need to say something soon if Paige didn't. At least she seemed calmer. Maybe she'd experienced another broken relationship. Over the years since Greg's death Paige had flitted from one boyfriend to the next with barely a breath in between, apparently her way of coping with her father's death, but her choice of boyfriends left much to be desired. Wendy tried not to judge. God loved all people equally, but she and Greg had held such high hopes for their children, and to see Paige taking up with men, who by their outward appearance alone, seemed to have such different values from those she and Greg had tried to instill in their children, caused Wendy concern.

She'd been especially alarmed when Paige had chosen a

Goth lifestyle. Wendy didn't even know what a Goth was at the time and had to look it up. Paige had begun dressing in black, she listened to dark music, slept a lot during the day and disappeared at night. But it wasn't just the lifestyle that concerned Wendy. Paige had seemingly set her Christian beliefs aside and was exploring alternate ones. But Wendy knew without a doubt that regardless of what Paige believed right now, God still loved her as His precious child and would never give up on her. And neither would she.

She reached out her hand and squeezed Paige's. "Feeling better?"

Paige raised her head and met Wendy's gaze. Her eyes filled again, and tears slowly trickled down her cheeks. When she spoke, her voice wobbled. "I'm...I'm pregnant."

Wendy's eyes widened. "Oh, sweetheart."

Paige gritted her teeth. "I don't want it."

Wendy passed her a tissue, more to give herself time to comprehend this unexpected news than anything. Paige took the tissue and wiped her face.

"How far along are you?"

"Thirteen weeks," Paige answered in a monotone voice.

"You've seen a doctor?"

She nodded.

"So it's definite?"

"Yes." Sitting back, Paige placed her hands on either side of her stomach. Wendy stared, still in shock. How had she missed seeing the baby bump? It was small, but because Paige was so thin, it was also obvious. "And you don't want it?"

Paige shook her head and sniffed. "I booked in for an abortion, but I couldn't go through with it." Wendy didn't miss

Paige's accusatory tone. No doubt she blamed her for her moral compass, but that was a good thing. It meant she hadn't completely forgotten everything she'd been taught. And being pregnant wasn't the end of the world.

Wendy squeezed Paige's hand. "I'm glad you didn't go ahead, darling. And I'm glad you've come home. We'll look after you." She hesitated. Would this mean that she and Bruce should put their plans to move on hold? Just that day they'd found several properties they were both happy with and they'd planned to prepare the house for sale in the coming weeks. How would Paige cope with that? Wendy drew a breath. Best leave that conversation for later.

Tears flooded Paige's eyes again. "I'm so scared, Mum. I don't want to be pregnant."

Wendy shifted along the couch and wrapped her arms around her. "It's okay, sweetheart. You'll be fine. We're here for you."

Paige sniffed again and rested her head on Wendy's chest. "Thank you." Her voice was little more than a squeak.

After a short while, Wendy suggested that Paige take a shower while she prepared her room. Not that it needed much preparation. She had moved out less than a year ago but had left most of her things in the room, including her bed. Wendy knew Paige had been living rough, but now that she was pregnant, she obviously understood the need to look after herself and her unwanted baby. It wasn't what Wendy had expected, but it was reality, and she and Bruce would be there for her. Even if it meant putting their moving plans on hold.

Paige agreed, and while she was showering, Wendy dashed upstairs to find Bruce. He was watching television in the living room. When she stopped in front of him, he turned the volume down and looked up. "Is everything all right?"

Sighing, Wendy shook her head. "She's pregnant."

"Oh." Their gazes met and held, and then his face curved into a small grin. "That means you're going to be a grandmother."

"Yes, but she doesn't want it."

His face paled. "She's not aborting it, is she?"

"No, but she was thinking about it. I don't know what she'll do, but I told her we'll be there for her. I hope you're okay with that, darling." Wendy held out her hand. Bruce took it and pulled her onto his lap, slipping his arms around her. "Of course it's all right. She's your daughter. It has to be all right."

"Thank you. I have no idea what will happen, but at least she's come home. She's in a real state. I didn't ask about the father, but I gather he's not involved, whoever he is. I'll get her cleaned up and then I'll make dinner."

"No you won't. I will. Or we'll order some in. Let me handle it." The warmth in his eyes echoed in his voice.

Wendy bit her lip. This was awkward. He just wanted to help, but Wendy doubted Paige was ready to face him. "Let me make her something simple. I think she'll want to sleep first, and then we can grab something."

"Okay, darling. You know what's best." He kissed the side of her head and then released her. "Let me know if I can do anything to help."

"I will. Thank you." She kissed him on the lips and then stood.

The shower was still running, so Wendy quickly went into Paige's room and checked the bedding. It was clean and made up as it had been since she left. There really was nothing to do apart from closing the curtains, which she proceeded to do. The room was how Paige had left it. A framed picture of her as a young girl holding her father's hand took pride of place on a shelf on her desk.

When Wendy picked it up and studied it, a lump grew in her throat. Where had all the years gone? It seemed like just yesterday that Paige was a little girl, and Greg looked so young. She didn't understand why God hadn't answered their prayers and saved him, but unlike Paige, she didn't blame Him. God was God, and His ways were higher than theirs. He obviously had a better plan for Greg. Nevertheless, knowing that didn't minimise her grief at losing him. They'd had such a happy marriage, and learning to live without him hadn't been easy.

She returned the picture to the shelf. Paige's university books still covered her desk. In fact, one was still open. Paige had never been overly committed to her Psychology course, but Wendy had been saddened when she dropped out of it altogether. She was a smart girl and could study and be whatever she wanted. Being pregnant obviously hadn't been a part of her plan. Wendy closed her eyes and recommitted the situation to the Lord. While being pregnant might not have been part of Paige's plan, she prayed for the little baby that was forming inside her. God knew it already. It might not have been His plan either, but God could make beauty out of ashes, good out of bad, and this little one would be precious in His sight, regardless of how he or she came about.

She didn't hear Paige come in behind her until she was right beside her. Wendy smiled. "Feeling better?"

"Yes," Paige replied. Wrapped only in a towel, she looked and smelled much cleaner.

"Let me find you some clothes."

"It's okay, I can find them. I think I'll just sleep, if you don't mind."

"That's perfectly fine, darling. Sleep as long as you want."

"Like forever?" Paige raised a brow as she unwound her hair from the towel wrapped around her head.

Wendy's eyes shot open. Surely she didn't mean...?

Paige sighed heavily. "It's okay. I won't do anything silly. Not that I haven't thought about it."

Wendy's jaw dropped. How could Paige have even considered such a thing? At least she hadn't followed through. *Oh Lord, how desperate Paige must be. Please comfort her, Lord. Let her see that she still has a future, even though she's pregnant.* Wendy rubbed her arm. "You'll get through this, sweetheart. Life will go on."

Paige shrugged. "Maybe. I just want it all to go away."

"You might see things differently after a good sleep."

"I doubt it." Paige crossed the room and opened a drawer. Pulling out a long black t-shirt, she slipped it on. It reached to just above her knees.

"Would you like something to eat before you sleep?"

"No, I'm fine thanks. I just want to sleep."

"Okay. Let me know if you need anything." Wendy went to leave, but then stopped. "Would you like me to dry your hair for you?"

Thinking Paige would say no, she was surprised when she nodded.

Wendy smiled. "I'll be right back." Dashing to the bathroom, she retrieved the hairdryer and some leave-in conditioner. She'd make the most of the opportunity to spoil and care for her daughter, because who knew how long she'd stay? At least while she was here, she could show love in a practical way.

Paige perched on the edge of the bed. Wendy sprayed her hair with the conditioner, running a brush through it before drying it. She needed a haircut, but she wasn't about to say so. Instead, as she brushed and dried it, she hummed some praise and worship songs and prayed blessings over her daughter and future grandchild's lives.

"There. Your hair is so soft and pretty." Wendy stood and smiled at her daughter.

"Thank you."

"You're more than welcome, sweetheart. Have a good sleep." She kissed the top of Paige's head, inhaling the smell of freshly washed hair.

"I'll try."

LATER, after Paige was sound asleep, Wendy sat with Bruce at the dining table. He'd gone out and picked up beef curry from the local Indian restaurant and divided it onto two plates. He extended his hand across the table, and after she took it, they bowed their heads. Her heart warmed when he prayed for Paige and the baby and asked God to bless both their families. He was such a good man, and she loved him with all her heart.

CHAPTER 4

*A*ll night, Wendy's mind whirled. As much as she trusted God to use Paige's unexpected, unplanned pregnancy to reach her daughter's heart, she couldn't get Paige's words out of her mind... *I don't want this baby, Mum.* Although it was still a tiny foetus, Wendy couldn't help but wonder if it sensed it was unwanted. The very thought grieved her. All babies were gifts from God, precious in His sight, but what would happen if Paige didn't change her mind? Would she and Bruce consider raising the baby as their own? It didn't seem right, not at their ages. If nothing else, it wouldn't be fair for the child to have old parents. Maybe Natalie and Adam would adopt it. Natalie said they'd like to start a family soon. But surely, they'd want their own. Could they find it within themselves to take Paige's baby and raise it alongside their own children? And if they did, would it always feel second best?

And what about the father? What if he was a drug addict or

an alcoholic? Would the baby be healthy, or would it be marred by the poor life choices of its parents?

Wendy knew she shouldn't worry, but in the middle of the night when sleep eluded her and thoughts swirled in her mind, anxiety knotted her stomach. She let out a heavy sigh as she stared at the ceiling. *Lord, I'm sorry. Please help me to trust You. Please settle my troubled heart and mind. You know how much I love Paige and how it grieves me to see her so distressed, and although this pregnancy was unplanned, it grieves me that she doesn't want the precious baby she's carrying. Lord, I pray that You'll soften her heart towards it, and that You'll help her to love it and care for it, even if she doesn't keep it. Protect the baby's heart and soul, and let it know that it's precious in Your sight, wonderfully and fearfully made. Unplanned, but loved all the same.*

A short while later, Wendy gave up trying to fall asleep and slipped quietly out of bed. Shrugging on her dressing gown, she tip-toed out of the room and pulled the door closed behind her. The house was in darkness, but motion-sensor lights popped on as she made her way along the hall, casting faint shadows on the walls. Stopping at Paige's door, she was tempted to check on her, but refrained. The last thing she wanted was to wake her when she obviously needed sleep. Instead, she continued down the stairs and into the kitchen. She headed straight to the kettle, turned it on and made a cup of tea.

She was sipping it slowly, deep in thought, when she heard a noise behind her. She turned her head and smiled. "What are you doing up, darling?"

Placing his hands gently on her shoulders, Bruce leaned over and kissed her cheek. "I could ask you the same question."

She reached up and grabbed his hand. "I'm sorry if I disturbed you. I couldn't sleep."

"It's okay. I was only dozing."

"Can I make you a drink?"

"Stay there. I can get it. Would you like yours topped off?"

She smiled gratefully and handed him her cup. "Yes, please."

Minutes later, Bruce joined her on the couch and slipped his arm around her shoulders. She snuggled against his chest while she sipped her tea. Lights flickered in the distance across the harbour; a faint sound of a siren broke the silence.

Bruce leaned his head against hers and gently rubbed her arm. "She'll be okay. She knows she'll be cared for here."

Wendy let out a slow breath and turned to face him. "I know, but I couldn't stop all these 'what-if' thoughts. I hate it when that happens. I had to get up."

"Well, it *was* a big surprise."

"You're not wrong. I've always thought Natalie would be the first to present me with a grandchild. Definitely not Paige." She met his gaze in the semi-dark. "What should we do about the house?"

He sighed. "It's not the best timing to be moving, is it?"

"No, but I was so sure we should. I think we should pray about it and then tell her what we were planning. See what she says. You never know, it might be the best thing for her. She could help you with the horses."

He let out a small chuckle. "It could be an ice-breaker."

Wendy took his hand and held it against her cheek. "I'm sorry she hasn't warmed to you."

"She'll come around eventually."

"I hope so. She can't go on forever blaming God for the changes that have taken place in her life."

"Well, she can, but let's pray she doesn't."

"Yes, of course you're right."

They prayed together, and then Bruce suggested they watch the sun rise on the deck.

Wendy laughed. "I was about to suggest we go back to bed."

Bruce waggled his brows. "Now, that's an invitation!"

She slapped him playfully on the chest. "To sleep."

"Oh." He pouted.

"Come on. Let's watch the sun rise then go back."

"Sounds good to me." Helping her up, he draped his arm around her shoulders, opened the sliding door, and walked with her onto the deck.

Wendy shivered in the pre-dawn chill and leaned closer to him. The sky was starting to lighten, and the lights across the harbour were fading. A light mist hovered across the water, giving it an ethereal look.

"You'll miss it, won't you?" he asked.

She nodded. "Yes, but I truly believed it was time. Now, I'm not sure."

"God must have laid it on your heart at this time for a reason."

She shrugged. "Maybe."

"Paige's pregnancy might not have been planned, but God knew she'd become pregnant and that she'd come home. Maybe He can reach her better on a ranch than a harbour-side home."

She lifted her face to his and chuckled. "We're not buying a ranch."

He stole a kiss. "*Hobby farm* doesn't have quite the same ring to it."

"You're right. We can call it a ranch if you want."

"We haven't bought one yet."

"When we do."

"We're going to miss the sunrise if we keep carrying on like this." Encircling her with his arms, he rested his chin lightly on her shoulder.

Wendy sighed with contentment. It was such a comfort to know she had Bruce's support. As the sky lightened further, she admired the sunrise that heralded a new day. The beauty of God's handiwork enveloped her, reminding her of His greatness. Her heart swelled with the knowledge that not only did she have Bruce's support, but the God of the universe was with them, and together, they'd get through whatever lay ahead.

AFTER WATCHING THE SUNRISE, she and Bruce returned to bed. She finally slept, but it was Sunday, and her alarm woke her not long afterwards. She turned it off and closed her eyes. It would be bliss to stay in bed. She began to drift off again, but then she remembered. Paige was in the next room. Pregnant. She hadn't even asked if she was suffering from morning sickness. No, she couldn't stay in bed.

Beside her, Bruce slept peacefully. Her heart swelled with love for him. She smiled to herself and then rose quietly. Passing Paige's door, she paused and listened. Nothing. Good. It meant she was sleeping. She headed for the bathroom and showered, and then returned to her room and began dressing for church.

Bruce stirred as she zipped up her skirt. He lifted his head and then sat and scrubbed his face with his hands.

"I'm sorry, darling. I didn't mean to wake you," she said.

He glanced at the clock on the bedside table. "Time I was up, anyway."

"You're right. I'll get breakfast ready while you shower."

"Thanks. Any sign of Paige?" he asked as he swung his legs onto the floor.

Wendy shook her head. "She's still sleeping. Well, I presume she is. I haven't seen her." She lifted the string of pearls Bruce had given her as a wedding gift and placed them around her neck.

"Let me help," he said. Standing, he quickly crossed the floor and took them from her. She met his reflected gaze in the mirror and smiled. Her heart fluttered. After he attached the clasp, he placed his hands on her shoulders and slowly turned her around. Encircling her with his arms, he drew her close and lowered his mouth. Her breath hitched as his lips brushed hers. She quivered at the tenderness of his kiss. Finally, she pushed him away. "We'll never get to church at this rate," she chuckled.

He smiled into her eyes. "I'm sorry. I find you difficult to resist."

"You're just a big softie." She flashed him a smile and then turned to recheck her appearance. She lifted her hands to adjust the pearls. They sat nicely around her neck and contrasted well with the light blue of her blouse. Grabbing her brush, she ran it through her hair while Bruce stood behind and watched. "Aren't you going to get ready?" she asked.

"Yes. But I love watching you." He stepped closer and rubbed her arms, nuzzling her neck.

"Oh, go on. I think you need a cold shower."

He laughed. "You're probably right. Okay, I'll leave you in peace." He popped a kiss on her cheek and then disappeared into their ensuite.

Wendy smiled to herself as she applied a light dusting of powder to her cheeks along with a touch of blusher. She was so blessed. Heading to the kitchen to make breakfast, she paused outside Paige's room. Still no movement or sound.

With no idea of what she'd feel like eating, Wendy kept it simple. Coffee and toast, with a poached egg for her and Bruce. By the time the coffee machine had produced three cups, and the eggs were poached and the toast made, Bruce appeared at the counter, looking and smelling fresh and clean. "Hi darling. Just in time." She smiled at him.

"Smells great. Can I help with anything?"

"You could set the table while I take a tray up to Paige."

"No problem."

Wendy put Paige's coffee mug and plate of toast on a tray and carried it up the stairs. She paused outside the door and tapped quietly. Nothing. She tapped again. Still nothing. Panic gripped her. What if Paige had done something terrible? Wendy shifted the tray to one hand and opened the door with the other. Paige wasn't there. Wendy almost dropped the tray as she hurried into the room. She set it down on Paige's desk and looked around. Her bed was cold, and all her things were gone.

CHAPTER 5

*W*endy hurried down the stairs, heart thumping. Bruce was carrying their breakfast to the table. Grabbing his arm, she panted, "Paige isn't here."

He turned to her and frowned. "What do you mean?"

"She's gone. Taken all her things."

"Did she leave a note?"

"Not that I could see."

"Oh dear. Shall we try calling her?" Bruce set the plates onto the table.

"We can, but I don't think her phone's working. It hasn't been for several weeks."

"Let's try anyway."

"Okay. I'll grab mine." She stepped into the kitchen and retrieved her phone from the counter and returned to the table. Sitting in her chair, she speed-dialed Paige's number and held Bruce's gaze, her heart pounding as she tried not to imagine the worst. It didn't even ring, going straight to a message advising that the phone wasn't in use and to try again later. "Nothing," she said, her shoulders sagging. A wave of uneasiness rose inside her like a swelling tide.

Bruce reached out and took her hand. "We'll find her, love. Don't worry."

She swallowed the lump in her throat and nodded. "I don't know where she would have gone."

"Natalie's?"

"I doubt it."

"Simon's?"

"Maybe, but I doubt that too."

"Let's call them both."

"Okay." She took a steadying breath and speed-dialed Natalie's number first. She answered on the first ring but said she hadn't seen Paige. Wendy then rang Simon's number. It rang, but he didn't answer. She reached his voice mail but ended the call without leaving a message. "I'll try again." This time, he answered sleepily after two rings. "Mum...what do you want at this time of morning?"

"Sorry, darling. Have you seen Paige?"

"No. What's wrong?"

Wendy grimaced. She couldn't break the news of Paige's pregnancy over the phone. "She was here last night but she's gone this morning without saying anything. We're worried about her, that's all."

"She can look after herself."

Wendy bit her lip. *Not in the state she's in...* "Maybe. She's not in a good way at the moment."

"Do you want me to look for her?"

"Would you know where to look?"

"I know a few places she might be."

"That would be wonderful, dear. Thank you. We wouldn't know where to start."

"It's okay. I'll call later and let you know if I find her."

"Thank you."

Wendy ended the call and set the phone on the table. "He's going to look for her."

When Bruce slipped his arm around her shoulder and gave her a hug, she couldn't stop the tears welling in her eyes. Where had the confidence she'd had while watching the sun rise just hours before gone? Just one hiccup and she was a weeping mess. Straightening, she grabbed a tissue and blew her nose. "I'm sorry. I feel so helpless."

"It's okay, darling. I'm sure he'll find her."

Wendy grimaced. "I'm not so sure. She knows how to disappear. I'm concerned she's going to hurt herself or the baby."

He took her hands. "Let's pray for her. God knows where she is and we have to trust Him to care for her."

She nodded and bowed her head while Bruce prayed.

"Dear Lord, we bring Paige before You. You know where she is and what state her mind is in. We ask that You be with her and prevent her from making decisions she might regret. We know how troubled she is, but Lord, we also know that You are the antidote to all of life's troubles. You can take her hurting, angry heart and soften it, heal it, and give her hope and a future. We ask now that she might be aware of Your presence, that she might know that she's loved, no matter what she's done, and that being pregnant isn't the end of the world. Please help Simon to find her and to bring her home safely.

And Lord, I pray that You'll give Wendy Your peace. Help us both to trust You in this and every matter. In Jesus' precious name. Amen."

Wendy wiped her eyes but left her head bowed as she allowed the peace of God to fill her heart. She knew God would see them through this, and she chastised herself for her weakness and asked God for forgiveness. *Let me draw on Your strength, dear Lord. I'm sorry for my weakness.*

'My grace is sufficient for you, for My power is made perfect in weakness.'

Yes, and I'm so grateful.

After several more moments, she raised her head and squeezed Bruce's hand. "Thank you."

"You're more than welcome, darling. Now, can I make you a fresh cup of coffee?"

"That would be lovely." She glanced down at the breakfast they hadn't touched. "I'm not sure what we'll do with the eggs."

"I think we'll toss them. I don't fancy cold poached eggs, but I can make some more toast. We should eat."

"We should. I hope Paige has eaten something."

"Try not to worry about her. I know it's because you care, but I believe that this is part of her journey to wholeness. I fully believe she'll come out the other side a stronger, better person. She's a smart girl. She's just troubled at the moment."

"You're so wise, Mr. McCarthy." Wendy smiled at him. "I do love you, you know."

He chuckled. "Yes, I do know. And I love you." He leaned forward and placed a gentle kiss on her lips. "Now, let me fix this breakfast."

"Thank you."

PAIGE ROLLED over on the piece of cardboard she'd found sometime during the night and rubbed her side. She hadn't slept like this for a while, and now she remembered why. It was horrid. The ground was hard and it was impossible to get comfortable, no matter how many layers of cardboard you could find. But she couldn't stay at Mum's. She wouldn't really want her there, even though she said she did. Not now that she was married again and had her own life to lead. A train rattled overhead, and around her, bodies stirred. If she was lucky, a good Samaritan might come by with some food. She really needed something to eat. This baby was making her hungry, and she'd already eaten the snacks she'd taken from Mum's pantry.

She pushed back the sob lodged in her throat. What was she to do?

An old woman with long, straggly hair and a missing front tooth hobbled by. "What are you lookin' at?" she hissed.

"Nothing," Paige retorted.

"Mind yer business, right?"

Paige pulled her meagre things closer and shivered. "I am."

The woman narrowed her eyes and hobbled on. A plastic bag, presumably holding all her worldly belongings, was slung over her shoulder.

Paige drew her knees up and wrapped her arms around them and began rocking. She had to devise a plan. If only she'd miscarry. She could live with that, but for some perverse reason, it seemed that only those who wanted their babies miscarried, as far as she could tell. She hadn't even suffered any morning sickness, so she figured the likelihood of miscarrying was low. God was punishing her. Paying her back for not talking to Him. If only she could wind the clock back. Take more care. How had she allowed herself to fall pregnant? She struggled to think of the men she'd slept with. Who was the father? *Stupid. Stupid.* She chastised herself over and over as she rocked harder and harder.

"Whoa there. You'll fall over if you keep that going." A large hand touched her shoulder, steadying her.

She glanced up. A middle-aged man with kind eyes smiled down at her. "Are you okay? Would you like something to eat?"

"If you're offering." Normally she would have refused, but her stomach had started to growl.

"I've only got bread, but it'll fill you up."

"Thank you." She took the bag he held out.

"You're welcome. Take care of yourself. Okay?" His voice was soft and caring and his kindness brought her to tears. "I'll try." She offered a small smile before he walked on.

The bread was stale, but it didn't matter. It was food. She ate three slices before she felt better. Now she needed the bathroom. Could she bring herself to squat in the dirt like a lot of homeless did? She'd done it before, but it wasn't something she liked doing. If she hurried, she might make it to the railway station. Stuffing the rest of the bread into her backpack, she stood and picked her way around assorted sleeping bodies until she reached the road where she came face to face with her brother.

"Simon! What are you doing here?"

He raised a brow. "More to the point, what are *you* doing here?"

"None of your business," she snapped.

"I think it is. You're my sister and you're sleeping rough."

"How did you find me? Did Mum send you?"

"A lucky guess. And I offered. Come on. Let's get you out of here." He placed a hand on her shoulder.

She shrugged it off. "I'm not going home."

"I don't care where you go, but you can't stay here."

"So where are you taking me?"

"To my place for a start."

"I'm not going to stay with you and your boyfriend."

"Have you got a better suggestion?" He raised a brow.

Paige folded her arms. "No."

"Well, you have two choices. Go back to Mum's, or come home with me. Andy won't mind."

Paige took a breath. "Does Mum know about Andy?"

His voice softened. "No, and I'm not in a hurry to tell her. She won't understand."

Paige shrugged. "You never know. But hey. I was on my way to the toilet. I'm busting." She pushed past him and scurried up the road.

He followed behind. "Why are you sleeping rough, anyway? Did that last dude you were with kick you out?"

"Something like that."

"Why don't you get a job? Then you could pay for a place."

"Can't get one," she called over her shoulder.

"Why not?"

"Dunno. No one wants me."

"You're not trying hard enough."

She turned around and glared at him. "Who gave you the right to judge me?"

"I'm not judging."

"Sounds like it." She huffed out a breath and then sprinted the remaining distance to the railway station. Early morning commuters were everywhere. She weaved around them and finally reached the ladies toilets. Rushing in, she found an empty cubicle, pulled her pants down and did the biggest wee she could remember doing, and she hadn't even been drinking much. This baby was doing crazy things to her body.

She sat for a while, not ready to face Simon again. She had a good mind to tell him to leave her alone, but she *did* need somewhere to stay. She sighed. Maybe she should go with him. Stay at his place until she figured something else out. Staying with him and his boyfriend had to be better than staying at Mum's. She couldn't handle being made to feel useless. Mum didn't mean it, but it was too much. It would have been better if she'd yelled at her and told her how stupid she was instead of telling her it would be all right and that she'd get through it. She didn't want it to be all right. She didn't want the baby, and she was sure Mum would try to convince her to keep it. That was never going to happen.

She stood and flushed the toilet. She couldn't stay there all day. When she emerged, Simon was leaning against the wall but straightened when he saw her. "So, what's it to be?"

"I'll come with you." The resignation in her voice made her cringe.

"Good. I'm parked not far from here."

She walked beside him. "Did Mum tell you anything?" she asked hesitantly.

"She said you were there last night but were gone this morning. She sounded worried."

Paige sighed with relief. No need for him to know just yet. "Good."

"Why? Is something going on?"

They reached his car, a snazzy red convertible he'd bought recently. "I still don't know how you can afford this."

"It's called a job."

"Don't be smart with me." She climbed into the passenger seat and buckled up.

"I'm not. It's true. If you work, you earn money and you can buy things. You can even pay rent."

"Well, listen to you, Mr. Know-it-all."

"What's going on, Paige? You're more cynical and prickly than ever."

"Nothing."

He turned his head as he slowed for a corner. "Really?"

She shrugged and nibbled her nails. Not that there was anything to nibble.

"Paige…"

She glared at him. "Mind your business."

"Tell me what's wrong." His tone softened.

She folded her arms and slumped in the seat. "I'm pregnant, all right?"

"You're what?"

"You heard."

"Why didn't you tell me?"

"Would it have made a difference?"

"I mightn't have been so short with you."

"That'd be a change."

"It's no wonder you have no friends. Listen to yourself."

"Like you're any different."

"I have friends."

"Yeah, right. *Boyfriends.*"

"Boyfriend, singular. Partner, actually."

"And you haven't told Mum?"

"No." He nodded to her stomach. "Does she know about…"

"That's why I was there."

"I thought you would have gotten an abortion. You're obviously not happy about it."

"I couldn't go through with it."

His head snapped around. "Well, well. Conscience get to you?"

"Something like that." She slumped in the seat and stared out the window.

"So, what are you going to do?"

"I don't know."

"I'll have to check with Andy, but I'm sure you can stay as long as you want."

"Gee, thanks."

"Don't burn your bridges, Paige. You're going to need someone to help you with this baby."

Paige sighed. He was right. She couldn't do this on her own, but did she want her gay brother and his boyfriend to be her support system? Honestly, she didn't know what she wanted. Ever since Dad died, life hadn't been the same. She'd been his little girl, and he was everything to her. Her hero. Her friend. But now, he was gone. He'd be so disappointed in her. *She* was disappointed in herself.

Simon's phone rang. They both looked at the caller's name on the dash and then at each other. *Mum.*

"Please don't answer. Give me time to think," she pleaded with him.

Simon's forehead creased. "She'll only want to know if I've found you."

"I know, but I need more time. Please."

He let out a heavy sigh. "Okay." He let it ring.

Mum left a voice message. The worry in her voice was palpable and tore at Paige's heart. She didn't want to hurt her mother, but she wasn't ready to face her again. To see the disappointment in her eyes.

"Will you let me send her a text, at least?" Simon asked.

"Can you wait for a bit?"

"All right. But I need to tell her you're okay soon or she'll be worried out of her mind."

"I know. I just need more time, that's all." Time for what, she wasn't sure. She'd like to disappear altogether, but Simon wouldn't let her do that. What she really needed was her father, but he wasn't there. But she *could* visit him. "Can we go and see Dad?"

Simon's head snapped up, his brow creasing. "Dad?"

"I know he's not there, but I want to feel close to him for a while."

"You really miss him, don't you?"

"Don't you?" She narrowed her eyes.

"Yes, but I try not to think about him too much."

"I think about him all the time."

"You were his favourite."

"Maybe. Anyway, can we go there?"

"I guess so." Simon pulled the car back onto the road and did a U-turn, squealing the tyres as he accelerated.

CHAPTER 6

While she waited for him to answer, Wendy prayed fervently that Simon had found Paige. Although he'd promised to call, she was anxious to hear from him. Bruce had said they should go to church, and she'd agreed, but she wanted an update before they went inside, or how else could she concentrate? Her heart was heavy as she tried not to imagine the worst, but it was so hard to stay positive with Paige so unstable. *God, please help him find her...*

The phone rang until she got his voice mail. She held Bruce's gaze while she left a message.

Bruce squeezed her shoulder. "Maybe he's driving."

Wendy gave him a perfunctory smile. "Maybe." But she remembered Simon telling her he had a hands-free set up in his new car, so there was no reason for him not to answer.

"Come on darling. Try not to worry."

"I'm trying. I just can't help this apprehension. I'm so concerned for her, Bruce. In her state, she could do anything."

"Do you want to go looking for her ourselves?"

Wendy sighed. "Other than wandering the streets of Kings Cross, I'd have no idea where to start looking. She never told us where she was living."

"Well, we have no choice but to pray that Simon is successful. Church is the best place for us right now."

She nodded. "You're right. Let's go."

Opening the door, she climbed out and took Bruce's hand. Heading towards the chapel, Wendy smiled and nodded at the other parishioners who were also headed in the same direction, but continued on. She didn't want to stop and talk, even though most were longtime friends. A member of this church since before she and Greg were married, she knew almost everyone, and although they'd offer to pray if she told them about Paige, she wasn't yet ready to share with them the situation, hoping and praying that Simon would find her and bring her home.

Natalie and Adam were seated three rows from the front on the left. Bruce stood aside and let Wendy go in first. Natalie looked up and smiled as Wendy shuffled along and sat beside her. Since her wedding, Natalie had gained a little weight and looked the better for it. Marriage was suiting her, and Wendy was pleased. Adam was a good man, although a little conservative, but he, too, seemed to have relaxed a little since their marriage. Wendy leaned over and hugged her daughter. "How are you, sweetheart?"

"I'm good, thanks. How are you? Did Paige turn up?"

"I'm fine, thanks. Just a little tired, and no, she hasn't turned up yet." Could Natalie see her concern? She bit her lip. She'd never been good at hiding her emotions. Maybe she should tell

Natalie. She and Paige were sisters, after all, and Natalie and Adam had looked out for Paige while Wendy was away and knew what she was like. But maybe it was up to Paige to tell them she was pregnant, not her. *When she was found.* No, she wouldn't say anything.

"Not sleeping well?"

"A lot on my mind, that's all."

Natalie frowned. "Like what?"

"I've decided to give up work."

"That's great. I'm glad you finally decided."

Wendy smiled. She'd been talking about it for some time, but making the decision to move had been the main trigger. Now there was a question mark over the move, but as she recalled Bruce's words of the previous evening, she wondered if God could indeed reach Paige better if she lived away from the city and all its distractions. All they had to do was find her and convince her to come with them.

The worship leader stood and invited the congregation to do the same. "Good morning, and welcome. Let's begin our service with some praise and worship. Please join me as we sing."

The band began to play one of Wendy's new favourites. She loved the old hymns, but the newer worship songs seemed to engender a deeper heart response to God, making it easy to praise Him and to be reminded of His absolute majesty and sovereignty in all things.

The Bible verse Pastor Jimmy based his sermon on was Philippians chapter four, verse seven, a verse she knew so well, but one which spoke to her heart anew. *"Do not be anxious about anything, but in everything, by prayer and petition, with thanksgiv-*

ing, present your requests to God. And the peace of God, which tran-scends all understanding, will guard your hearts and your minds in Christ Jesus." By the end of the service, Wendy had her thoughts under control, at least for now, and peace filled her heart, despite still not knowing Paige's whereabouts. Worry was something the devil used to take her focus off Jesus and achieved nothing other than weighing her down. She knew that, but she'd certainly needed the reminder.

While drinking coffee in the hall next door, her phone pinged. The urge to check it was overwhelming. She pulled it from her purse and glanced at the message. It was from Simon.

Hi Mum. Found Paige. She's okay-just talking to her. Will be in touch. Simon.

Relief washed over her. She shared the message with Bruce. "Told you she'd be all right," he said, winking.

She chuckled. "You did."

"Something I should know about?" Natalie asked, peering over her shoulder.

Closing the message, Wendy shook her head. "No, not yet, anyway."

"Sounds intriguing. What are you hiding, mother dear?"

"Nothing," Wendy replied defensively.

Natalie raised a brow. "It doesn't seem like nothing."

Wendy sighed. It wasn't fair to keep Natalie in the dark altogether. "Okay. I told you we were looking for Paige?"

"Yes…"

"Well, Paige actually stayed with us last night but was gone when we got up this morning, and we were worried about her. Simon said he'd try to find her, and he just sent a text saying he had."

"Is she in trouble again?" Natalie asked. While Wendy was overseas, Paige had been charged with being drunk and disorderly in public, and Natalie had bailed her out.

"No, nothing like that."

Natalie narrowed her eyes. "Something's going on. I can tell."

Wendy grimaced. "You're right. Can't hide anything from you, can I?"

"No, not really. So...?"

"I'll leave it to Paige to tell you. But pray for her, sweetheart. She's mixed up and she needs Jesus."

"Okay, I won't press any further. I'll pray for her. I hope she hasn't done anything stupid."

"So do I, sweetheart. So do I."

THEIR FATHER WAS BURIED at the cemetery on the other side of the harbour, not far from their family home. Crossing the harbour bridge, Paige gazed out the window at the Manly ferry chugging out of Circular Quay, horn blasting and smoke billowing into the clear, blue sky. She'd never forget her childhood trips on the ferry to the seaside suburb of Manly. When she was little, Dad would lift her up on his shoulders so she could see over the timber railing and wave to all the people on the small boats as they passed. She could still taste the salt on her lips when the ferry plunged into the rollers crossing the heads and sea spray drenched them, making them laugh. She closed her eyes as pain squeezed her heart afresh.

Her baby would grow up without a father. Or a mother.

She couldn't keep it. What kind of life could she give it? Not that she wanted to keep it. But a strange, unexpected thought surfaced, confusing her. What would it be like to take her child, her flesh and blood, on a ferry ride? To show it new things, to hear its laughter and joy? She quickly banished the thought. She wasn't keeping it.

Ten minutes later, Simon parked the car in the car park of the Northern Beaches Cemetery. After Dad died, she'd come here often, mostly on her own, and mostly without her mother's knowledge. Sometimes she stayed all day when she should have been at Uni lectures or doing assignments. The others wouldn't approve. They would have said it was weird, macabre, but she'd been drawn to her father's grave like a bee to honey. Maybe it was the Goth influence, but she found visiting his grave comforting, even though under the earth all that remained was a skeleton.

Since moving out, she hadn't been here. Living rough in Kings Cross on the other side of the harbour made it too difficult. She felt bad, as if she'd let him down. "Have you been here at all since he died?" she asked her brother.

"No. I prefer to remember him as he was."

"Do you want to come with me?"

"No. You need time on your own."

"That's unusually sensitive of you." She gave him a wry look.

"I'll accept that as a compliment."

She shook her head, let out a small laugh, and opened the door. The whoosh of a strong nor'easter almost knocked her off her feet. The cemetery, perched on the side of a hill above the ocean, was often blustery, but this was crazy. Steadying herself, she walked down the pathway, battling the wind, until she reached Row 567, then turned left. Dad's grave was the third one on the right. Her gaze, as always, was drawn to the granite headstone.

Gregory Jonathon Miller
Born 15th June 1956
Passed from this earth into the Father's arms 22nd September, 2013
Sadly missed by his wife, Wendy, and three children, Natalie, Simon and Paige.
'Blessed are the pure in heart, for they shall see God.'

PAIGE KNEW the words by heart, but they angered her. He was only fifty-seven, in the prime of life. Why did God take him then? She wasn't stupid. People died all the time, but she couldn't understand why there were so many verses in the Bible promising that God would answer the prayers of the faithful. The verses were totally misleading. The whole family, along with the whole church, had prayed fervently that Dad would survive his heart attack, but God had turned His back on them. Ignored them. Dad died, and everyone seemed to accept it as God's will. Except her. Once, she'd accepted that He was a God of love, but not anymore. What kind of God would give their child a stone when they asked for bread? That's what the Bible said. *If you, then, though you are evil, know how to give good gifts to your children, how much more will your Father in heaven give good gifts to those who ask him!* That was such a lie.

She sat beside the grave and picked at the grass. If Dad had lived, she wouldn't be in this mess now. She'd still be at Uni and she wouldn't be pregnant. She'd really stuffed her life up. "If only you were here to tell me what to do, Daddy. I'm so sorry for disappointing you and Mum. For letting you down. I miss you so much." A hot tear rolled down her cheek. "I don't want this baby, but I can't get rid of it either. You taught me too well." Her voice faltered. "What am I to do?"

Drawing a long, deep breath, she wiped her cheek with her hand and gazed out at the ocean while wind whipped strands of hair around her face. In the distance, a large cruise liner headed out to sea, and soaring just above the cliffs, sea gulls caught the updraft and then suddenly dove into the water before emerging again to do it all over again. Life went on. But what if you didn't like your life? She'd tried being a Goth. True Goths said you didn't *become* one, you *were* one. For a while, she'd fit in, but deep down she knew she hadn't been born a Goth. For her, it was an escape, nothing more. She didn't know what she was or what she wanted. She didn't fit anywhere. She was drifting, and she knew it. But it was one thing to drift when it was just you, but now... She looked down at her stomach and gulped. Why had she been so careless?

She blew out her breath and squeezed her eyes shut as sobs she couldn't stop wracked her body.

For I know the plans I have for you...plans to prosper you and not to harm you, plans to give you hope and a future.

Goose bumps prickled her skin. If only that were true, but how could it be? She felt a restlessness in her soul, but pushed it away. God didn't have a plan for her life.

Eyes blurring with tears, she hugged Dad's gravestone. "I'm so sorry, Daddy. I'm so sorry."

A hand rested on her shoulder, and Simon crouched beside her. "Are you all right, Paige?"

She shook her head and fell into his arms. "No, I'm not all right."

"What can I do?"

"Nothing." Her voice drifted in the wind.

He held her until her sobbing subsided. "I think you need Mum."

She nodded. He was right. She needed Mum. He helped her up and they walked back to his car. "I'm sorry."

"It's okay. You were having a meltdown. It's allowed. But you need to sort yourself out, for the sake of the baby, if nothing else."

"I know. But I'm so scared. I'm not ready to be a mother."

"You'll make a great one if you give yourself a chance."

"You really think so?"

"I know so. You're smart, and underneath your tough exterior lies a heart of gold. I remember what you used to be like. It's still inside you, Paige. Go home and find yourself. That's what Dad would have wanted."

Fresh tears stung her eyes. Could she really do that? Could she really find herself? Discover who she was, who she was meant to be? She didn't know, but she had no option. She'd do it for Dad.

CHAPTER 7

$\mathcal{W}$armth radiated through Wendy as she pulled Paige to her chest and kissed the top of her salty head. "I'm so glad you've come home, sweetheart." She smiled at Simon over the top of Paige's dark, messed up hair and gave him a grateful nod.

Simon was still an enigma to her, but when she needed him, she knew she could rely on him. If only he'd talk to her. She knew so little about his private life these days. It was like he was keeping secrets from her. But he'd found Paige and brought her home safely, and for that, she was truly grateful.

Paige hung her head. "I'm sorry, Mum. I shouldn't have left like I did."

"It's okay, darling, although we were worried about you. Have you eaten?"

"A little."

"Would you both like lunch?" She looked first to Simon, who nodded, and then at Paige, who also nodded.

"I picked up some fresh rolls at the bakery on the off-chance you'd stay. I'll get it ready while you freshen up. Or would you like a cup of tea first? Or something else?"

"Stop fussing, Mum," Simon said. "We can look after ourselves. We know where the kettle is."

Wendy bit her lip. "Of course you do. I'm sorry. I'll just look after lunch." She laughed lightly.

"I'd love a nap," Paige said, stifling a yawn while pulling away. "I'm feeling tired all of a sudden."

Wendy was tempted to ask where she'd slept last night, but refrained. Wherever it was, she obviously didn't get much sleep. "Rest, darling. I'll call you when lunch is ready."

"Thanks, Mum. I think I will. I'll curl up on the couch, if that's all right."

"That's fine. You might need to move Muffin, that's all." Wendy's large, fluffy Persian lounged all day and night on the couch and only shifted when it was dinner-time or to curl up on her lap.

"I'll sort him out."

"I'm sure you will." Paige held no great fondness for the cat.

Wendy glimpsed Bruce moving from the sun room where Paige was headed and wondered what the interaction between the two would be like when they faced each other. Paige had chosen to have little to do with him, avoiding him whenever possible, so Wendy was pleasantly surprised when she heard Paige say hello as they passed. It wasn't much, but it was a start.

When Bruce reached her and Simon, he extended his hand and shook Simon's. "Thanks for findin' her. Your mother was mighty worried."

Simon responded with a knowing smile and a nod. "I know what she's like."

"It's only because I care. I don't worry normally," Wendy defended.

Simon and Bruce shared a smirk.

"Stop it, you two, or I won't feed you."

"She knows the way to a man's heart," Bruce said playfully, winking at her.

She laughed. "Go on, you two. Do something while I get lunch."

Bruce sidled up to her and slipped his arm across her shoulder. "Sure you don't want help, darling?"

"It's nothing fancy, I'll be fine. Go and do something manly."

"Manly?" Bruce asked, laughing. "Any suggestions?"

Wendy shrugged. "Look at the tools in the shed. See if Simon wants any. I don't know. I'm sure you'll think of something."

"As long as you don't need help."

"I don't. Off you go." After shooing them out of the kitchen, she released a breath. Men! But she loved them both. She prayed they'd get to know each other a little and that God could use Bruce over time to draw Simon back to Himself. He had such an easy-going nature. Maybe Simon would warm to him since he kept her at arm's distance.

It grieved her that out of her three children, only Natalie had kept her faith as they all grew into adulthood. Occasionally she asked herself what she'd done wrong, especially when other families she knew still worshipped together. Not that church attendance equalled a relationship with God, but it was something. Simon and Paige point blank refused to go. All she could do was pray for them and love them unconditionally, even if their lifestyles sometimes filled her with despair. She had to hold onto hope, for without hope, what was there?

With the men gone, she went about preparing a simple lunch. A pre-cooked quiche, a tossed green salad, and the rolls from the bakery. She checked on Paige. Seemingly asleep, it'd be a shame to wake her for lunch. Wendy's heart went out to her daughter once more. A rocky road lay ahead, of that she was sure, but she was so glad that Paige had returned and was at home, at least for now. They'd have to take a day at a time. Paige was capricious at the best of times. Who knew what she'd be like now that she was pregnant?

Leaving Paige to sleep, Wendy grabbed plates and cutlery and set the table on the deck. It was a glorious spring day and the harbour sparkled below. Being a Sunday, pleasure crafts of all sorts cruised the calm waters of the protected cove. Some had thrown out an anchor and a fishing line, while others puttered along, leaving small wakes that sent ripples ashore. The drone of jet skis spoiled the serenity. Wendy sighed. She'd miss the harbour when they moved, but she definitely wouldn't miss that horrible noise.

Returning to the kitchen, she smiled when Bruce and Simon came back from whatever manly thing they'd found to do. They were still chatting together easily. "Ready for lunch?"

"Yes, please," Bruce said, his eyes twinkling. "Can we help?"

"You can help me carry it to the deck." She handed him the quiche and Simon the salad. She took the rolls and condiments. Passing the sunroom, Wendy looked in again on Paige. Her eyes fluttered and opened.

"Lunch is ready, sweetheart. Would you like to join us?"

Paige swung her legs off the couch and sat. "Yes, I'm really hungry."

"That's what happens when you're pregnant," Wendy said softly. She guessed that Paige knew little about what was happening to her body and what to expect as her pregnancy progressed. If she'd been considering having an abortion, Wendy suspected she wouldn't have been taking care of herself or the baby.

"I'm not looking forward to being fat," Paige said as she stood, rubbing her stomach. Her baby bump wasn't visible under her loose shirt, but she was obviously conscious of it.

"It's not forever, and I think you'll be a bean pole with a balloon out front." Wendy laughed.

"Mum! That sounds horrible!"

"Sorry, love. I'm sure you'll look wonderful."

Paige pursed her lips but didn't respond.

"Come on, let's join the others."

Paige followed her outside. Bruce and Simon were already seated and looked up. She hesitated, but then sat a little awkwardly opposite Bruce. Wendy understood how uncomfortable this must be for her. Paige had had little to do with Bruce and was still angry about losing her dad. But if anyone could put her at ease, Bruce could.

Wendy caught his gaze and raised a brow ever so slightly. He got the message.

"Shall we give thanks?" he asked, holding out his hands.

Wendy didn't miss the look that Paige and Simon shared, but they complied and joined hands anyway. Seeing their hands joined warmed her heart so, although she knew they were only doing it out of duty and expectation, not because they had a personal relationship with the Lord. But every bit helped, so she offered her thanks silently while Bruce offered his out loud. As always, his prayer was heartfelt but gratefully short.

They raised their heads and Wendy began to serve.

"It's okay, Mum, we can help ourselves," Simon said as he took two rolls from the basket, placing one on Paige's plate and the other on his.

Bruce squeezed her hand under the table. He knew how anxious she was to make them feel at ease, but she had a tendency to mother them just a little too much. She returned his squeeze and tried to relax. "How's work going, Simon?"

"Good. Busy as usual." After quitting University several years earlier, he was now the area manager for a convenience store chain. "I'm thinking about studying part-time next year."

Wendy's eyes widened and a smile grew on her face. "That's wonderful, dear. What are you going to study?"

"Business. The same course I started before. I can now see its use."

"I'm so glad to hear that. You'll have far more opportunities once you're qualified."

"Yes. It's taken me a while to realise that. I like my job, but I don't want to be stuck there forever."

Paige squirmed in her chair. No doubt she thought she was stuck already.

"How will you manage with work as well as study?"

He shrugged. "I'll study at night."

She smiled. Going back to school was great, but she hoped he wouldn't bury himself in work and study and forget to socialise. He hadn't had a girlfriend for some time. It didn't overly bother her, but it did seem a little unusual.

"Can I get anyone a drink?" Bruce asked.

"I'd love an iced tea," she replied, holding his wrist lightly.

"Make that two," Paige added. "Although I'd rather have a beer."

"It's not good to drink while you're expecting, sweetheart," Wendy said. "Iced tea's a good choice."

Paige sighed heavily and leaned back in her chair.

"Simon?" Bruce raised a brow.

"I'd love a beer, too, but I guess I'll have a Coke if you have one."

"Coming right up." He stood and walked inside.

With Bruce gone, Wendy studied her two children. She'd love to speak honestly with them and share her heart, and her hopes and dreams for them both. Her heart ached for them to come back to the faith they'd grown up with, but she had to be patient and trust that God was working in their lives. They were adults and could make their own choices about how they lived, but they were missing out on so much by not choosing to have Jesus as their Lord and Saviour. Instead, she smiled and said how lovely it was to have them both there. "We need to do this more often."

"I guess I'll be doing it every day for a while, if you'll have me," Paige said offhandedly while she buttered her roll.

"Of course we will, sweetheart. You can stay as long as you want." Wendy rubbed her back. "There's something we were going to run past you both."

They looked up. "Spill the beans, Mum. What's up?" Simon asked.

She took a deep breath. Maybe she should wait for Bruce to return, but she'd started now, so she continued. "We're thinking of selling the house and moving onto acreage. Bruce would love to get some horses, and I think I could do with a change. It might do you good, too, Paige." Wendy placed her hand lightly on Paige's wrist.

A look passed between her and Simon that Wendy found hard to gauge. "What do you think?"

Paige blinked. "I don't know. You've taken me by surprise."

"You always wanted a horse," Simon said pointedly.

"Yes, but that when I was little and Dad was around."

"A change might be good for you. Get you out of the city for a while," Simon continued.

She shrugged. "Maybe. I'll have to think about it."

He leaned back in his chair and returned his attention back to his mother. "It doesn't bother me, so if that's what you want to do, do it."

"You'll have to collect your boxes. They've only been stacked in the garage for, how long?" Wendy gave a small chuckle. She'd been trying to get him to take them for years.

"Ah, so that's why you're moving! To get rid of my boxes."

"Something like that." She laughed lightly.

Bruce returned with the drinks and set them on the table. They all offered him their thanks.

"Mum told us you're moving." Simon spoke matter-of-factly, as if he didn't care. She wondered if he ever thought of the past. He rarely spoke of it, not even about his father. It was like he'd left it behind and had moved on. So unlike Paige who'd let it drag her down. Losing a parent was hard and they all handled it differently. She prayed that over time they'd be able to talk about their loss openly. Greg needed to be remembered. He was their father, after all.

Bruce raised his brow at Wendy.

"I hope you don't mind, darling. We were chatting and it seemed the right time to run it by them."

"That's fine." He smiled as he took his seat. "So, what do you think?" He looked first at Simon and then at Paige.

"It doesn't affect me," Simon responded. "I think it could be good, but Paige isn't so sure."

"That's understandable. It was unexpected. Anyway, we can talk about it more later. It's just a thought at this stage."

"We looked at a few places yesterday," Wendy said.

"Really? What did you find?" Simon asked, seemingly more interested than Paige.

"We went out to the Hills District and found a couple of properties that looked great. But it's early days. We have to get this place ready for sale first."

"I can help," Simon said. "I can probably enlist a friend to help, too."

"That's nice of you to offer, dear. That'd be great, thank you."

"How much is there to do?"

Wendy looked to Bruce. "I'm not sure. Bruce has been painting and doing bits and pieces here and there while I've been at work. Oh, and that's another thing... I've decided to stop work."

"Mum! After all these years!" Simon exclaimed. "What will you do with yourself?"

She chuckled. "I'm sure I'll find something. Especially living on acreage." She turned to Paige. "You're being very quiet, sweetheart. Are you okay?"

"I'm not feeling too well. I think I'll lie down."

"Okay, no problem. I'll check on you shortly." Wendy smiled at her as Paige pushed her chair out and stood. She'd barely eaten anything, even though she said she was starving.

When she left, Wendy turned to Simon. "You don't have to say anything if you feel you shouldn't, but where did you find her?"

Simon grimaced. "She probably wouldn't want me to say, but I will. She was sleeping with the homeless under a railway bridge at the Cross."

Wendy sucked in a breath. "Oh dear. That's terrible. How did you know where to find her?"

"She's called me from there before. I guessed that's where she'd be. You're going to have your work cut out with her. I suggested she stay with me and... and my house mate, but I think she'll be better off with you. If she'll stay. She told me she's pregnant."

"Yes. She's such a worry, but I'm glad she's come home. We'll do our best, won't we, darling?" Wendy turned and caught Bruce's gaze.

He nodded. "Yes, we will. Thank you for bringing her here."

"You're welcome," Simon replied.

"Did...did she say who the father is?" Wendy asked tentatively.

"I don't think she knows."

"That's what she said." Wendy sighed heavily. It grieved her greatly that Paige had let her morals slip so much that she didn't even know who the father was. And then there was the risk of disease. "It's sad. The baby will never know its father."

"I guess it'll survive without one," Simon said. "But she said she doesn't want it."

Wendy grimaced. "She might change her mind."

"I'm not so sure. She sounded determined. Does Natalie know?"

"Not yet," Wendy replied. "I thought Paige should tell her."

"Don't let her leave it too long. I'm thinking it might be best if you tell Natalie."

Wendy sighed. "You might be right. She might feel left out otherwise."

"Yes. I'm surprised she and Adam aren't here now."

"They're having lunch with his parents."

"Right. Well, I'd best not stay too long. Andy will be wondering where I am."

"Your housemate?" Wendy tilted her head.

"Yes."

"I'd like to meet him. You've been sharing the house for a while now. You must get along well."

"We do. I'll bring him over one day soon."

"Do that. And thanks once again for finding Paige. We really appreciate it."

"You're welcome."

They finished their meal and Simon left soon after. After he left, Wendy made a pot of tea and she and Bruce sat and looked at the view while they drank it.

"Our life will never be the same, my darling. Are you sure you're okay with having Paige stay with us?" she asked.

"Yes, I'm sure. If she were my daughter, I'd want her cared for. We can't let her sleep on the street."

"No, we can't. I just pray that she'll be happy both here and at the new place."

"We'll do everything we can to see that she is."

"Thank you, Bruce. I love you so much."

"And I love you." He leaned over and pulled her into his arms, and that's how they stayed until the jet skis started up again.

CHAPTER 8

*T*he next day, Paige slept so much that Wendy grew concerned. "We need to get you to the doctor for a check-up, and we also need to get you booked into the hospital."

With no enthusiasm, Paige agreed, and so, the following day, Wendy accompanied her to the doctor. She didn't voice her concerns over the baby's wellbeing, because maybe it was completely fine, but she had a feeling that something was wrong. Maybe she was just being over anxious. Hearing that Paige had slept rough before, and not knowing who the father was or what he, or Paige, for that matter, had been involved in when the baby was conceived, all sorts of anxious thoughts festered. It was better to know for sure than to imagine the worst.

Dr. Anderson had been the family's doctor for many years, but she wasn't a gynaecologist. Wendy thought that starting with a familiar face might be the best way to go, and Dr.

Anderson would refer them onto whoever she felt was the best health care professional for Paige. She and Bruce had already agreed to cover the costs since Paige had no money. It was a slippery slope, because once started, it would be difficult to know when to stop supporting her. But since an innocent child's life was involved, they felt strongly that Paige needed the best care available.

Sitting in the reception area, Paige completed the medical questionnaire and then was unable to sit still while she waited to be called. A number of others were also waiting. A mother with two small children, one of whom appeared to be running a temperature by the colour of his cheeks, an elderly man chatting to an equally elderly lady who had trouble hearing him, and a much younger, smartly dressed woman. The television was playing the local morning show.

Paige stood and walked to the water dispenser and carried the plastic cup filled with water back to her seat. Drank it. Stood and got another. Tossed the cup into the bin. Went to the bathroom. Tapped her fingers on the arm of the chair.

The consulting room door opened and everyone looked up. A young woman, possibly about the same age as Paige, stepped out, lowering her gaze as she walked past the waiting patients and made a bee-line for the exit. Her cheeks were damp and she looked downcast. Although she didn't know the woman, Wendy prayed silently for her.

The young mother with the two children was called next. Pushing to her feet, she held the toddler with the inflamed cheeks in her arms and motioned for the older sibling to follow.

Paige slumped in her chair and folded her arms. "How much longer do I have to wait?"

"I think you're next. Be patient, sweetheart." Wendy took her hand and squeezed it. "Are you okay?"

Paige shook her head. "No."

"Do you feel sick?"

"No. I just don't like doctors."

"You'll be fine. Dr. Anderson is a lovely doctor, you know that. You've known her all your life."

Paige shrugged and picked at her nails. She'd only been to the doctor once about her pregnancy, when she had it confirmed. Wendy had decided not to say much for fear of alarming her, but she suspected that Dr. Anderson would give her a full check.

Finally, her turn came. Wendy offered a smile of encouragement. "I'll wait here, sweetheart. I hope all goes well." *I'll be praying for you.*

While she waited, Wendy prayed silently for Paige and the baby. Memories of sitting in this very waiting room when she was pregnant with all three of her children flooded back. Unlike Paige, she'd been elated, filled with anticipation and wonder at the new life growing inside her. But she and Greg were happily married, young and in love. As far as Wendy knew, Paige had never been in love. She'd had numerous boyfriends, but they came and went as often as the Manly ferry chugged in and out of Circular Quay. She had no one, other than her and Bruce, and possibly Simon and Natalie, to share the journey with. Not that being alone and pregnant was totally unusual, but nevertheless, it saddened her.

Wendy's phone rang. From the ring tone, she knew it was

Natalie even before she pulled it from her purse, and wondered why she'd be calling now. Natalie was a school teacher and should be with her class of six-year-olds. Answering quietly, she asked Natalie to hold until she walked outside, not wanting to disturb the other waiting patients.

She gestured to the receptionist and then pushed the door open and stepped outside into the sunshine. "Sorry, darling. I'm at the doctor's and didn't want to disturb anyone. How are you?"

"I'm good. More to the point, how are you? Are you unwell?"

Wendy grimaced. Despite Simon encouraging them to do so, she and Bruce still hadn't told Natalie about Paige's pregnancy, and Paige had been less than enthusiastic about telling her herself. Wendy guessed that feeling she'd failed, she'd rather not have her big sister cast judgement on her. Not that Natalie would do that, but she was 'Miss Perfect' according to Paige. But now, the time had come, whether Paige liked it or not.

"No, I'm fine. I'm here with Paige."

"What's wrong with her?"

"She's pregnant." There was no easy way of saying it.

"Pregnant?" Wendy could hear the utter surprise in Natalie's voice.

"Yes. I've brought her here for a check-up."

"Who's the father?"

Wendy bit her lip. Saying Paige didn't know who the father was spoke volumes about her lifestyle, opening the floodgates for judgement to be cast. She couldn't lie, however. "She hasn't said, but whoever he is, he's not involved."

"How is she?" Concern, not judgement, sounded in Natalie's voice.

"Mixed up. Unhappy."

"I can imagine." Natale sighed. "I'll come over."

"Aren't you at school?"

"I took the day off. I had some appointments, and I thought we might catch up over lunch."

"That would be lovely, dear. It's been a while since we've had a girl's lunch date. I'm not sure how long Paige will be. I'm guessing she'll need blood tests and maybe a scan, but she won't need to do them straight away."

"I...I was going to tell you that we're about to start IVF. We probably shouldn't talk about it with Paige there."

"Oh, darling. I had no idea. How are you feeling about it?"

"Mixed. We wanted to conceive naturally, but it just isn't happening."

"But you've only been married less than a year."

"We've had tests. It's unlikely to happen."

"Oh." She didn't want to ask what the problem was. She didn't need to know. "Well, I'll be praying it's successful."

"Thank you."

"It must be galling to hear that Paige is pregnant."

"It took me by surprise." Natalie blew out a breath that was loud enough for Wendy to hear. She could only imagine how Natalie must be feeling. To want a baby and not be able to conceive, and to hear that her wayward sister was now expecting, but wasn't happy about it, would be a challenge for anyone.

"God will bless you, dear, in His time."

"I hope so." Natalie's voice was laced with emotion. Wendy wished she was there to give her a big hug.

"Come over whenever you're ready. Let's meet at The Harbour View Café."

"Okay. It's going to be interesting having lunch with Paige."

"Yes." Wendy chuckled. "She's already given me more grey hairs in the last day or so than I care to admit."

"Sounds like you're going to need a bucket of dye."

"Possibly." Wendy chuckled again and then grew serious. "We're praying that God will touch her life through this. She seems so lost."

"It might be just the thing she needs. You never know."

"Yes. Anyway, I must go, darling. I'll let you know if we're held up."

"Okay. See you soon."

Wendy slipped her phone back into her purse and paused before re-entering the medical centre. More than ever, she needed God's wisdom to handle this situation. Two daughters. So, so different. But she loved them both, and God loved them, more than she ever could. *Lord, please bless my girls. Draw Natalie closer to You as she embarks on this journey, and please work in Paige's life and let her see and experience how deep Your love is for her and her baby.*

When she stepped inside, Paige was standing at the reception counter and turned to face her. Her eyes were red as if she'd been crying. *Lord, give me strength for whatever lies ahead...*

CHAPTER 9

*N*atalie sat opposite Paige at The Harbour View Café. If her faith wasn't as strong, she could easily have thought how cruel fate was. Here was her younger sister, who'd caused the family so much grief, having a baby she didn't want, while she and Adam, who'd done everything by the book, were starting fertility treatment. It didn't seem fair, but Natalie was determined not to be bitter. Paige was troubled, but she was also carrying a precious little baby who shouldn't be a victim.

"Have you been keeping well?" she asked.

Paige shrugged. "I haven't been sick, if that's what you mean." She twiddled a strand of her long, dark hair between her fingers. Last time Natalie had seen her, it had been pink.

"Well, that's good."

"The doctor wants to check me for STD's." She said it to shock, but Natalie wasn't surprised. Paige's lifestyle didn't reflect the Christian morality she'd been raised with, and

Natalie knew she was loose with whom she slept. It wouldn't surprise her if Paige did have a sexually transmitted disease.

"It's best to be checked, just in case." Natalie glanced at their mother as she sipped her water. Mum didn't deserve this, but Natalie knew she'd look after Paige. *If Paige let her.* Mum loved her so much and was deeply concerned over her lifestyle and the fact that she'd shunned God and her faith. But God wouldn't leave Paige alone. When she was just a child, Paige had asked Jesus into her life. So passionate about Him, she was always the first to pray at family devotion times, always ready first for church, and always asking others if they knew Jesus. Somewhere deep down, that little girl still existed.

In her child-like faith, even though she was a teenager, Paige had expected God to heal their father. She'd trusted Him implicitly and couldn't understand why He didn't save him. He was supposedly all loving, kind, and powerful, but in her eyes, He'd let her down. Bitterness and disappointment festered. Paige stopped attending church. She grew cynical and distant. Then she dabbled in other lifestyles, and so began her downward spiral. And now she was pregnant. If that didn't make her wake up, Natalie wondered what would. God had work to do in her life, but that was His specialty. Offering the broken, the bruised, the disillusioned and the hurting the opportunity to be free of all that weighed them down.

None of them knew why He'd chosen not to let Dad live. They wouldn't know that until they met Him face to face in eternity, but His ways were higher than theirs, and this life was just a stepping stone to the next. Trusting Him, regardless, was something Paige couldn't grasp. She'd wanted what *she* wanted. Of course they all wanted Dad to live, but Paige hadn't been able to forgive God for not answering their prayers, even when Mum reminded her that God was sovereign and it didn't mean He loved them any less. He'd just answered their prayers differently.

The next few months were going to be interesting and challenging. Natalie prayed then and there that God would give Mum the strength and wisdom she'd need to support and care for Paige. To show her love. God's love. And that Paige would let go of her bitterness and open her heart anew to Him as her baby grew inside her.

Paige let out a heavy sigh. "The doctor said the baby is okay from what she could tell."

Natalie smiled. "Well, that's good news."

"I guess so." Paige sounded resigned, not excited. If only she knew what a privilege it was to be carrying a precious new life, whether it had been planned or not.

The waitress arrived and stood before them, pencil poised. "And what can I get you ladies today?"

"I'll have my usual, thanks. Chicken Caesar salad and a flat white," Mum said, smiling. "Have you girls decided?"

Natalie quickly perused the menu. "I'll have the pizza, thanks." She ignored the look Mum gave her. She couldn't help it if she had a weakness for Italian food.

"And what would you like to drink?"

"Oh, sorry. I'll have a cappuccino, thanks."

"Perfect. And what would you like?" She raised her brow at Paige.

"I'm not hungry."

Mum frowned and tapped her on the wrist. "You said you were starving earlier. You need to eat something, darling."

Paige scowled. "All right, if you insist." She let out a sigh and looked at the waitress. "Do you have hamburgers?"

"Yes, we do. Would you like a plain or gourmet one?"

"Plain, with chips, thanks."

"You're welcome. And to drink?"

"Juice."

"Okay ladies. I'll bring your meals out shortly."

Mum smiled. "Thank you."

Once the waitress left, nobody spoke. Finally, Mum broke the silence. "How's Adam doing with his study?" Natalie assumed she'd asked that question to get the focus off Paige. Adam was studying for his Master's in Education. A teacher, like her, he wanted to get a promotion to school principal one day, but to do that, he needed a higher qualification.

"Good," Natalie replied. "He's so smart and diligent."

"I know he is. I hope he's finding time for you as well." Mum held her gaze. Before their wedding, Natalie had shared her doubts about marrying Adam with her mother. They didn't have the affectionate relationship that Mum and Bruce did, and she'd wondered if they were truly suited. Recalling their recent vacation to the Whitsunday's, where romance had certainly not been in short supply, she felt her face flush. "Yes, he's keeping everything in balance."

"That's good to hear, especially when..." Mum stopped herself and glanced at Paige, her cheeks flushing.

"Especially when what?" Paige asked.

Mum mouthed the word *Sorry...* Natalie hadn't wanted to tell Paige about her fertility treatment, but what it did it matter? She'd find out eventually, and it might make her think.

"Adam and I are about to start fertility treatment. We're having trouble conceiving."

Paige shrugged nonchalantly. "Have mine."

Natalie blinked. "You...you can't mean that, Paige. Once you have the baby, it will be different. I'm sure you'll want to keep it. But it's a lovely offer, thank you."

"I'm serious. I don't want this baby. I was going to abort it, but I couldn't do it, but that doesn't mean I want it."

"Don't make any hasty decisions, Paige. Things can change, so let's wait until closer to time. But of course, if you truly don't want the baby when the time comes, Adam and I would seriously consider raising it, but I'd need to talk with him."

"Obviously. But it would solve both our problems."

"It could, but it's a huge decision."

Natalie glanced at Mum. She was keeping quiet, no doubt as surprised as she was. Paige seemed so serious, but Natalie was sure she'd regret giving her baby up. And what if she and Adam decided to adopt it, and then Paige wanted it back? How would the child cope when it discovered the truth? And what if the fertility treatment worked and she fell pregnant? Would she and Adam cope with two babies? Would it be fair to Paige's baby? So many things to consider and pray about. The main consideration was that the baby was loved. If Paige truly didn't want it, maybe she and Adam *could* become its parents, but wow, there was a lot to think about.

The waitress arrived with their meals and drinks. They all smiled politely and thanked her. The waitress nodded and scurried off to take orders from another table. Natalie was glad for the interruption to the conversation and used the opportunity to steer it onto less contentious issues. "How's Bruce going with the painting?"

Mum look flustered and blew out a breath. "Good." Blinking, she rubbed her cheek. "I've got news for you, too."

Natalie frowned, curious. "Go on."

Mum glanced at Paige and lightly held her wrist. What was going on? What other news could there possibly be? Mum shifted her gaze back to Natalie. "We've decided to sell the house and move onto acreage."

"Wow! That's great, Mum. Whereabouts?"

"Somewhere in the Hills District. Bruce is excited."

"I can imagine. But what about your work? It's a long way to commute."

She smiled. "I'm finishing at the end of the year."

Natalie blinked, gob-smacked. "I don't believe it. I thought you'd never leave." Her mum had been so dedicated to her work that Natalie expected her to still be there when she was a hundred.

"Neither did I, but things are different now. I'm looking forward to spending more time at home."

Natalie chuckled. The change in her mother since she'd met Bruce was nothing short of amazing. It warmed her heart to see her so content and in love after years of grieving for Dad. God had indeed blessed her. "And what about you, Paige? Will you go with Mum and Bruce?"

She shrugged. "I've got nowhere else to go."

"Well, that's not quite true. You could stay with Adam and me, and I assume Simon would have you."

"I don't want to stay with him and his boyf...housemate."

Paige's gaze quickly cut to Mum. Was she about to say *boyfriend?* A chill ran through Natalie. Was their brother *gay?* A lot of questions would be answered if he was. He hadn't had a girlfriend for a long time, and he never invited the family to his place. He was so secretive about his private life and his friends. If he was, Mum would be shocked. Devastated. Had she picked up on Paige's slip of tongue? Natalie remained still, praying she hadn't. Seconds passed. Seemed like minutes. Focused on her salad, Mum said nothing. Natalie breathed a small sigh of relief, though she wasn't sure if Mum had heard and was simply blocking it out. Natalie turned to Paige. "Well, I'm sure you'll enjoy living on acreage. You might get that horse you always wanted."

"Maybe." Paige shrugged again before taking a bite of her hamburger.

"So, Mum, what are the plans?" Natalie asked, still trying to digest what she thought she'd heard about her brother.

Mum finished her mouthful of salad and then replied, "We have to tidy the house up. Simon offered to help and said he'd bring his housemate with him. Once it's ready, we'll put it up for sale and then seriously look for the right place. It'd be nice to be moved by Christmas. Did I tell you that some of Bruce's family is coming for the holiday?"

"I think you did. Nate, Alyssa and the children. Is that right?"

"Yes, and Aiden's also thinking of coming."

Natalie didn't miss Paige's momentary flicker of interest. She smiled. "That will be nice for Bruce. He must be missing his family."

"He is. We're planning a trip to Texas sometime next year

once we're settled into our new place. But our plans might change now."

"Why?"

Mum took Paige's hand and squeezed it. "It all depends on this one."

"Don't change your plans because of me. I can look after myself." Paige sounded defensive. It was admirable that she wanted to be independent, and Natalie hoped Paige would mature and be able to look after herself properly sometime soon, but right now, she needed Mum. She had nothing, and emotionally, she was a wreck.

Mum smiled. "We'll see, sweetheart. Anyway, we're looking forward to moving. I hope you're okay with it, Nat. I'm sorry we didn't tell you earlier."

"It's okay, Mum. I'm excited for you. And Adam and I will help as well."

"Thank you, darling. I appreciate that."

"It's the least we can do." Natalie smiled and glanced at her phone. "I need to head off soon, sorry."

"Another appointment?" Mum asked.

Natalie nodded. "Yes. The dentist. I thought I may as well get everything done today since I was already taking it off."

"Good idea. I hope you get the all clear."

"So do I." Natalie finished her coffee and then pushed her chair back. "Well, it's been an interesting lunch."

"It has indeed," Mum said. "It's been lovely seeing you. Take care, sweetheart." She squeezed Natalie's hand, smiling sweetly.

Natalie stood and gave her a kiss and a hug. "I will." She

turned to Paige and placed her hand on her shoulder. "And you, missy, take care of that baby. I'll be praying for you."

Paige stiffened. Maybe it was the wrong thing to say, but Natalie wanted Paige to know she wasn't alone. That she was part of the family, and that she was loved. She rubbed Paige's skeletal back. "Let me know if you need anything, okay?"

"I won't, but thank you," Paige replied off-handedly.

Natalie left and walked to her car, her heart heavy with concern over her sister and the baby. *And her brother... wow... who would have thought? Lord, give us wisdom to deal with this. Please.*

CHAPTER 10

Several days later, Paige returned to the doctor to get the results of her tests. This time, she went alone. Mum had wanted to come, but she needed some space. Mum and Bruce had been hovering over her like she was a helpless child. She wasn't a helpless child. She knew it was only because they cared, but it was almost too much. She'd contemplated getting a job and a place on her own, but while she might be able to work now, what would happen in a few months' time, when she was heavily pregnant? How would she afford to keep a place of her own then? In the end, she decided to stay with them, but to do things on her own. She could even apply for a casual job. That way, she wouldn't be letting her employer down when she had to stop work. But today was the day she'd find out if either she or the baby had any problems.

Her heart rate kicked up a notch when her name was called. Although she didn't want this baby, she didn't want it to be deformed, either.

"Paige, how are you?" Dr. Anderson asked, waving her into the consulting room.

Paige slumped onto the chair beside the doctor's desk. "Fine, I guess."

"That's good to hear. I've got your results back."

Paige couldn't tell by the doctor's tone whether she was about to convey good news or bad. She straightened. Took a slow breath. Her heart was thumping. It was strange that she cared this much. Although she had no desire to keep the baby, a little girl, so she'd discovered when she had her scan, having made the decision not to abort it, she'd started to feel a level of responsibility for it. For *her*.

"We have some good news. You're clear of any diseases, however, you're further along than you thought. You're actually eighteen weeks, and that makes your due date the end of January.

Paige did a quick calculation and swallowed hard. She now knew who the father was. *Colin Daley.* The dude who'd dumped her for another girl.

"The baby is quite small for eighteen weeks and I'm a little concerned about her development. I'm going to refer you to a gynaecologist who specialises in at-risk pregnancies."

She said it so matter-of-factly, but Paige knew the doctor was referring to her drug and alcohol use. No. *Abuse.* How had she let herself get sucked into that kind of lifestyle? Dad would have been so disappointed. But since discovering she was pregnant, she'd stopped everything, although it hadn't been easy. She guessed that showed she cared a little about the baby.

"Here are the details. Call to make an appointment as soon as you can."

Paige took the referral and went to stand.

"Before you go, have you got any questions?"

Paige shook her head. "Not really."

The doctor dropped her professional tone. "The baby will be fine if you look after yourself, Paige. I know your mother will help in that regard, but make sure you eat well and get enough sleep." She smiled. "Cheer up. Having a baby isn't the end of the world. Have you thought any more about what you might do once you deliver?"

Paige drew a breath and released it slowly. "My sister and her husband might adopt her."

"Natalie?" The doctor's eyes widened.

Paige nodded. "I suggested it to her the other day."

"Wow. Okay...I guess that could work. But I still think you should consider keeping her. You might regret it if you don't."

"I don't think I would, but I guess things can change."

"They certainly can. Anyway, I'll look forward to hearing what you decide. Even though you'll be under Dr. Simmons's care now, feel free to see me whenever you want, even if it's just to have a chat."

"Thank you. I'll keep that in mind. You've been very kind." Paige stood and gave the doctor a small smile before leaving.

Out on the street, she turned left to go home, but paused, and then chose instead to wander along the strip of shops that lined the busy road, pausing occasionally to look in the window, although, with her mind elsewhere, she had little interest in what was inside. In many respects, she would rather have not known who the father was. Knowing it was Colin Daley changed everything. Should she tell him? At one time she thought she loved him. He'd treated her well to begin with.

He was a pretty cool dude, a real Goth. A thinker. He'd pushed her to examine her own beliefs and prejudices, and for a time, she'd liked that. Having walked away from her Christian faith, she'd found a new freedom in having no rules and in doing whatever felt right, but she'd always sensed he wasn't as committed to the relationship as her. When he brought home another girl to share not only their flat but their bed, she'd realised she didn't feel comfortable with no boundaries. With no moral compass. He didn't like it when she told him he had to choose. He chose the new girl and told her to leave.

Her gut told her no, she shouldn't tell him. She wasn't stupid. If he returned to her, it would only be because of the baby, and she knew a relationship wouldn't last. But then, didn't he have a right to know? Didn't the baby have a right to know who her father was? She let out a heavy sigh. It was all too hard. Wiping a tear from her eye, she trudged on.

"Paige?"

Turning, she looked into a slightly familiar, friendly face. "Robyn?"

"Yes. How are you, dear? Long time no see." A good friend of her mother, Robyn had been like a close aunt to Paige and her siblings when they were young.

"I'm...I'm fine, thanks. How are you?" How could she say otherwise? But she was anything other than fine.

"Really well. So, what brings you back to these parts? Visiting your Mum?"

"I've actually moved back home for a while."

Robyn's face lit up. "I'm sure your mother is pleased about that."

Nodding, Paige hid a sigh. "Yes. Kind of."

"Would you like a coffee? I was on my way to the café."

Paige hesitated, but then accepted her offer. Robyn had always been someone she felt comfortable with. She wasn't sure why, but Robyn never seemed to judge.

Soon after, sitting in one of the small cafés that dotted the strip, Paige found herself sharing her situation with Robyn. The older woman said little. She just listened as Paige told her about her unwanted pregnancy, the lifestyle she'd fallen into, and how she hated disappointing her parents, especially her dad, even though he was no longer here.

After their second cup of coffee, Robyn shared her story. "I had an unwanted pregnancy when I was a little younger than you are now."

"Really?" Paige leaned forward. This was news. Robyn had been single as long as she could remember. She vaguely remembered Mum saying she'd been married once, but as far as Paige knew, she didn't have any children.

Robyn nodded and toyed with her cup. "Yes. When I was young, I played the field, for want of a better word, and I fell pregnant."

"I had no idea. What did you do?"

Robyn sighed and leaned back in her chair. "I had the baby, but decided to adopt it out."

"Did you ever regret that decision?"

Robyn blew out a breath. "At the time, it was the right thing to do. I was unmarried, I was a student, and I wasn't in a position emotionally or financially to be caring for a baby. But later, when Neil and I couldn't have children, yes, I came to regret giving my baby up. But it was too late to change anything." She reached out and took Paige's hand, stroking her skin with her thumb. "You have to do what's right for you, Paige. No one can tell you what that is. They don't have to live with the consequences of your decision. These days it's easier to keep your baby, but only if it's truly wanted, because nothing is worse than an unloved child. Not that I think for a moment you wouldn't love your baby, but you know what I mean."

Paige nodded.

"The best thing you can do is pray about it. I know you've strayed from your faith, but the little girl I remember used to pray about everything. God will guide you if you let Him."

"Just like He answered our prayers about Dad?" Paige pursed her lips. She shouldn't have said it, but it was what she thought.

"I know you're angry with Him for letting your dad die, but believe me, God truly does care. It's just that His ways are higher than ours, and He sees things differently to how we do. Your dad is waiting for you in the life to come. The one that lasts forever. Just make sure your name is in The Book."

Paige rubbed the back of her neck. *The Book...* The memory verse she'd learned when she was eight floated back. *Nothing impure will ever enter it, nor will anyone who does what is shameful or deceitful, but only those whose names are written in the Lamb's book of life.* Well, she was cooked. She'd done plenty of shameful and deceitful deeds. May as well accept she'd never see Dad again. "I'm not sure I believe any of that anymore."

"Don't close your heart to God, Paige. He truly does care for you, even if you can't see that right now. Anyway, I must go. It's been lovely catching up, and please call me if you ever want a sounding board. I promise I won't tell you what to do. I'll just be a good listener."

Tears sprang to Paige's eyes. It was great talking to someone who knew exactly how she was feeling, even if she talked about God. She sniffed, brushed her eyes. "Thank you."

Smiling, Robyn stood and opened her arms. "Come here. Give me a hug."

Paige stepped into her arms and sobbed into her chest. She hadn't meant to, but she yielded to the emotion that had been building for weeks and let it release in a torrent.

Robyn held her close and rubbed her back."There, there, sweet girl. It'll be okay, you'll see." Kissing the top of her head, Robyn prayed quietly for her, and something shifted deep inside Paige. She thought it was her stomach having a convulsion, or her heart beating in response to Robyn's prayer. But then it dawned on her. Her baby was moving!

CHAPTER 11

Slipping her arm around Bruce's waist, Wendy admired the freshly painted rumpus room. Having decided to sell the house, they'd both agreed that the room needed a face-lift since the crazy purple that Paige and Simon had painted it when they were teenagers might not appeal to a prospective buyer. "It looks so much cleaner and brighter, doesn't it?" She lifted her face and smiled.

"It certainly does." He lowered his face towards hers and kissed her gently. Pulling away, he gazed into her eyes. "You know what tomorrow is?"

She nodded. "The anniversary of our meeting."

He trailed a finger down her hairline. "So, let's plan to do something special. Just you and me."

The thought of doing something special filled her with anticipation. "That sounds lovely. What did you have in mind?"

"Oh, I thought we could sneak away for the weekend.

Somewhere in the mountains, perhaps? Or the beach. Whatever you'd prefer."

"That sounds wonderful, but I'm not sure we should leave Paige on her own. She's so up and down at the moment. Maybe we could just go out for the day."

A look of disappointment flashed across his face. "Can't Natalie keep an eye on her?"

Wendy pondered for a few moments. "It's certainly a tempting suggestion. I'll ask her."

"It seems a long time since we were on our own. I know it hasn't been, but I miss having you to myself." He brushed her cheek with the back of his hand.

Tingles ran through her body. Having Paige to care for was a privilege she didn't take lightly, but she also shouldn't neglect her husband. She didn't want to. "You know, Paige is a big girl and I think she can look after herself for a weekend. We can't molly coddle her."

"Absolutely. So, where would you like to go?"

She thought for a moment. Both options appealed, but then she decided. "Since it's spring, let's go to the beach."

He smiled. "Done deal. Any beach in particular?"

"Avoca's my favourite. There are some lovely apartments on the hill that have terrific views of the ocean. Plus, I love walking around the headland."

"Sounds good. I'll book something now." He frowned. "So, is that north or south of here?"

She chuckled. "Sorry. It's north."

· · ·

THE FOLLOWING DAY, after packing the car and giving Paige some last-minute instructions, they headed north along the M1 towards the Central Coast. Although heavy, the traffic on the three-lane motorway was flowing, and seated beside Bruce, listening to the latest Michael Bublé CD, Wendy began to relax.

"I had a phone call from Nate yesterday," Bruce said casually, tapping his fingers on the steering wheel in time with the music.

"Oh. What did he have to say?"

"Just confirming details for Christmas. He wanted to know what the plans are."

"Did you tell him we don't know?"

"I did. I told him we've decided to move, so we don't know where we'll be."

"Maybe we should rent a holiday house."

"At the beach?"

"Yes, why not? The kids will love it."

"Good idea. Let's look at some places this weekend."

"Sounds great." Wendy let out a small sigh. "The only problem might be Paige, since she'll only have a month before the baby is due."

"Do you think she'd come?"

Wendy shrugged. "I don't know, but we have to assume she will."

Moments passed and Wendy's thoughts turned to Paige and the baby. The gynaecologist was a little concerned about the baby's size but said that as long as Paige ate a healthy diet and took good care of herself, the baby should be fine. There were no other issues that she could see. The main thing that concerned Wendy was Paige's emotional and mental state. She was unstable and lacked direction.

"Do you think she'll keep the baby?" Bruce asked.

Wendy let out another sigh. "I don't know. She certainly hasn't been as adamant about putting it up for adoption these past few days, but I don't think she knows what she wants." Wendy turned her head and studied her husband's profile. He'd been amazingly understanding and supportive since Paige had announced her pregnancy, but they needed a break. Caring for her and preparing the house for sale had been all consuming. "Let's not talk about her right now. We need a break. It's called respite." Reaching out her hand, she placed it lightly on his thigh, smiling when he entwined his fingers with hers.

"I like the sound of that," he said softly.

"It's hard to believe it was only a year ago that you spilled coffee on me. I'll never forget the look on your face."

He threw his head back and laughed. "And I'll never forget the grin on yours that you tried unsuccessfully to hide."

Wendy shook her head but laughed with him. "I was never any good at poker."

"And that hasn't changed. But it's what I love about you. It seems surreal sometimes, but here we are, Mr. and Mrs. McCarthy of Cremorne, Sydney."

"Soon to be land owners in the Hills District." She laughed again.

He grew serious. "Are you absolutely sure, my darling? If you're not one hundred percent convinced it's the right thing to do, don't do it for me."

She squeezed his hand. "I'm sure. I'm looking forward to having a place that's truly ours."

He smiled. "And so am I."

A SHORT WHILE LATER, after stopping to buy some local fruit at a roadside stall, they arrived at the Seaview Apartments at Avoca Beach. Perched on a hillside overlooking the sparkling ocean, the complex was a recent addition to Avoca's line-up of modern holiday accommodations. In years gone by, Wendy, Greg and the children had often stayed in a small cottage near where these apartments now stood. The cottage, small but quirky, held many happy memories. The children's delighted squeals as they stood impatiently outside the door waiting to burst inside to choose their beds. The distinctive smell of jasmine growing along the fence. Traipsing, tired and sunburned, up the hill after a morning on the beach. Such happy times. But Greg was gone, the children were grown, and the cottage no longer existed.

Standing on the deck, with a light breeze blowing her hair, she turned and lifted her face to Bruce's. How blessed and thankful she was to have him in her life. Their relationship had been so unexpected, but so fulfilling and wonderful. She couldn't have wished for a better man to share her life with.

"What are you thinking, darlin'?" He lifted a hand and trailed his fingers along her temple while gazing into her eyes.

"Just how much I love you, that's all." She placed her hand gently over his and drew it to her lips. They needed this time alone to rekindle their love. Not that it had waned, but she was very aware that she'd been neglecting him of late.

He pulled her close and hugged her, resting his forehead against hers. "Let's go inside."

STANDING at the kitchen counter waiting for the kettle to boil, Paige ran her hands over her growing belly. Tears welled in her eyes. Since feeling the baby move inside her, her resolve to give it away had weakened, but the thought of raising a child on her own terrified her. Although Mum and Bruce had said she could stay as long as she wanted, it wasn't the same as having a partner to share the experience with. She didn't want to be a single parent. Despite her rebellion, she still held the belief that all children should have a mother and a father, like she and her siblings had until Dad died. Was it fair to keep a baby when she had nothing to offer it?

You have love to offer...

Paige blinked. Love wasn't enough. And who said she had love to offer? She didn't feel very loving.

I can help if you let Me...

Pursing her lips, Paige wiped her eyes angrily and made her cup of tea. She wasn't on talking terms with God, and if that was His attempt to get her back, He may as well forget it. She slumped onto the couch and put her legs up. Her belly protruded, reminding her afresh of her predicament. How could she get through the next twenty weeks? She was already going stir crazy. She had to do something, but what?

As she considered her options, including returning to University if they'd have her, her phone rang. It was Natalie.

With Mum away, no doubt she was checking on her. She let out a heavy sigh. Why did everyone think she needed constant minding? Annoyed, she answered it. "Natalie. Checking on me?"

"You don't have to be so defensive all the time, Paige."

"Sorry." She sat up and sipped her tea. "What do you want?"

"I thought you might like to join us on a picnic since it's such a lovely day."

"Who's going?"

"Just Adam and me, and a few of our friends."

"Church friends?"

"Yes…" Natalie replied hesitantly.

"I don't think I'll go."

"They're not going to preach at you, Paige."

"Maybe not, but won't I embarrass you?" She flicked on the television.

"Not if you're polite."

"I can't promise anything."

Natalie tutted. "Come anyway. Stop being so childish."

"What if I had other plans?"

"Do you?"

Paige bit her lip. "No."

"Okay then. We'll pick you up in half an hour. Be ready."

Paige let out a resigned huff. "Okay."

NATALIE WAS true to her word, and half an hour later, she and Adam arrived to collect her. Determined to try to be nice, Paige met them with a smile. It felt fake. It was a lot easier to be argumentative and annoying. Maybe it was a sibling thing, because she'd spoken civilly with Robyn.

"How are you feeling?" Natalie asked after hugging her.

"All right, I guess." She shrugged off-handedly and then gave Adam a hug.

"You're looking good," he said.

"Thank you. Though I'm not sure I believe you."

"You look better than when I last saw you."

"Well, I guess that wouldn't be hard." She rolled her eyes. The last time she'd seen Adam was at Natalie's birthday party. She'd drunk too much and passed out on their couch.

"It must be Mum's cooking," Natalie said.

"Maybe." Paige shrugged. "So, where are we going?"

"Lane Cove National Park."

"I haven't been there in a long time."

"Neither have we. It should be lovely this time of year."

Paige climbed into the back of the car and fastened her seat belt. Adam and Natalie did theirs up in the front. She wondered if Natalie had told Adam she'd offered them her baby. Nothing was said about it. They made small talk all the way, as if they were treading on egg shells with her. They said nothing about their fertility treatment. But then again, she wouldn't expect them to.

They arrived at the turn-off to the park and drove slowly along the winding road that led past numerous picnic spots along the river. Stopping at the designated area, Paige tried not to groan when a group of twenty-somethings looked up and waved. From a quick glance, they all seemed to be couples. Great. She should have stayed home.

She got out of the car, ensuring her loose top covered her

baby bump. Harking back to her Goth days, she was dressed in black, a colour she thought might help disguise her pregnancy.

Natalie introduced her to the group. They all greeted her with friendly smiles and hellos. One of them, Angela, was obviously pregnant. In fact, Paige thought she might burst at any moment. She groaned. One day soon, she'd look like that.

Adam set a chair on the grass for her beside Natalie. She thanked him politely. They offered her a cool drink and homemade cookies. She accepted both with a smile she hoped appeared genuine. The group chatted together as if they'd known each other forever. They tried to include her, but when asked what she did, she had no answer other than saying she was still trying to figure that out, but that she might go back to Uni. Natalie's head tilted at that comment.

The day passed. The group shared their food and everyone seemed comfortable in each other's company. It was too much. Soon after lunch, Paige excused herself and went for a walk. The water flowed slowly along this stretch of the river that wound its way from the city through suburbia. Bordered by trees and pockets of picnic areas, you'd never know the city was just a stone's throw away. It was a peaceful oasis. A young couple drifting along in a row boat raised their hands and waved. Without thinking, Paige waved back.

The path weaved around some giant gum trees and then led back to the river. A large rock ledge jutted out over the water. She made her way to it and clambered up, sitting down with her legs stretched out in front of her. The sun warmed her back, but inside, her heart was cold. Why did she even entertain the thought that she could give her baby a good life? Natalie and Adam's friend, Angela and her husband, Dave, would be great parents. They were eagerly looking forward together to the birth of their first baby any day now. Adam and Natalie would also make fantastic parents, given the opportunity. Paige had nothing to offer a child, not even love. She didn't know what love was anymore. Not since Dad died and bitterness took hold in her heart. No, she had nothing to give. She'd give the baby up for adoption. Natalie and Adam could have first option. She wouldn't waver anymore. That way, she could start planning her life. After the baby was born, she'd return to Uni, get a job and move out. Maybe even do some travelling if she could save enough. Normal things any twenty-three-year-old might do.

With that settled, she stood and returned to the group. Some were still sitting and chatting, while others, including Adam, kicked a ball around on the grass. She joined them.

Adam hurried to her side and asked if she should be playing. She said that as far as she knew, there was no rule about not exercising while pregnant, and the thought of sitting and chatting again didn't appeal. He shrugged and told her to take care.

"I will, don't worry."

The exercise did her good. It pleased her that she hadn't forgotten how to kick a ball, although she became breathless after sprinting to retrieve it from the bushes. When had she become so lazy? At school, she'd been on all the sports teams. Swimming, netball, rowing, volleyball, even water polo for one term. She'd often won awards and represented her school and district at the state titles for swimming and netball. But everything changed after Dad died. Everything. She hadn't handled his death well, she knew that, but maybe it was time to rebuild her life. She might not ever forgive God, but she could regain her fitness, finish her degree, and start enjoying what life had to offer. Make Dad happy.

With that sorted, she also decided to make a serious offer of her baby to Natalie and Adam on the way home.

CHAPTER 12

$\mathcal{N}$atalie unpacked the picnic bag in silence while Adam rinsed the plates and put them in the dishwasher. Paige's offer to adopt her baby had come as a bombshell to Adam. When Paige had suggested it earlier, Natalie hadn't mentioned it to him, assuming that Paige wasn't serious. But today, when they dropped her back at Mum's, she'd spoken to them in a very adult manner.

"I've made my decision. I'm not going to keep the baby, so if you would like first option to adopt her, let me know."

Natalie's heart was torn. She desperately wanted her own baby, but how could they turn down this offer? The baby girl would be her flesh and blood, her niece, but could become their daughter if they both agreed. And there was no guarantee the fertility treatment would work. Adam's sperm count was so low the doctor held little hope of her falling pregnant, although they hadn't shared that news with anyone.

After emptying the bag, she turned to face him. "What are

you thinking, sweetie?" They'd been married almost a year, and their marriage had been everything she could have hoped for. Just prior to their wedding, she'd had cold feet. Adam was a good man, stable and hard-working. It was his strong faith that had drawn her to him, but when she saw the loving, affectionate relationship her mother and Bruce had, she began to wonder if she and Adam would ever experience such romance. Maybe her mother had spoken to him, although she'd never asked, because since their wedding, he'd brought her flowers at least once a week, took her to dinner often, and showered her with love. Her initial misgivings of having a marriage devoid of romance had been unfounded. The only thing missing was a baby. And he was blaming himself for that.

He ran his hand over his short, dark hair. "I'm not sure. It came as a huge surprise. I don't know what to think."

Stepping closer, she placed her hands on his chest and met his gaze. "We don't need to make a decision right away. Let's pray about it."

"Good idea. I guess I'm worried she'll change her mind."

"There's always that possibility. Anyway, it's something to consider."

Pulling her close, he rested his head against the side of hers. "It sure is."

AFTER NATALIE and Adam dropped her home, Paige decided to paint her room. Mum had mentioned it might be good to freshen it prior to putting the house on the market, so now was the perfect time. How hard could it be? She moved her furniture into the middle of the room, not an easy feat and one she questioned was a good idea half-way through moving her desk. But she did it anyway.

She pulled her posters off the walls, took down the curtains, and found some old sheets to place over the furniture and carpet. Having watched Bruce paint one of the other rooms, she knew she had to wash the walls and tape up the edges. After washing one wall, she gave up and called Simon. He and Andy weren't doing anything and arrived within the hour to help her.

Hearing the car pull up outside, she ran downstairs to open the door for them. The two men shared a joke as they walked up the step. Paige didn't miss the look of affection that passed between them.

She'd met Andy once before and thought then what a pity he wasn't available. Strong and handsome, he reminded her a little of Aiden, Bruce's youngest son whom she'd spent some time with in Fiji at Bruce and Mum's wedding. Andy wasn't effeminate in any way, and the thought crossed her mind that she could easily fall for him if he wasn't gay and she wasn't pregnant, but he and Simon were close and she doubted that would change.

She still struggled to accept her brother being gay. Dad would have been disappointed, and Mum would be horrified when she found out. As would Natalie. It was almost worse than her being unmarried and pregnant. She and Simon were certainly giving her family plenty of challenges.

"Hey, sis. Your help has arrived." Simon smiled as he leaned forward and kissed her cheek. "You remember Andy?" Turning around, he placed his hand lightly on Andy's shoulder.

"Yes. Thanks for coming." She smiled at them both.

"You're welcome." Andy's voice was soft and smooth, and when their gazes met, something moved inside her. It could have been the baby, but she thought it was more likely her heart. She chastised herself. It was wrong to be attracted to her brother's partner. Very wrong.

"Come inside." She stepped aside to let them pass and then followed them into the house. "Would you like a drink?"

"No, we're good. You'd better show us what you're doing so we can get started." Simon headed to her room. "What made you think you could do it on your own?" He sounded incredulous.

She shrugged. "I thought I could. I had no idea how hard it would be."

He shook his head. "Okay. Tell us what to do."

"I've washed one wall, but I couldn't keep going. It wore me out."

"I'm not surprised. You're getting fat, sis." He chuckled and made a face at her.

"Don't be rude."

"I'm not. It's a fact. Have you decided what you're doing?"

"With the baby?"

He nodded.

Conscious of Andy's presence, she was cautious with her reply. "Not sure yet, but I'm thinking I'll adopt it out."

"Probably wise. I can't imagine you being a mother." He grabbed the sponge and began washing the back wall, unaware that his words were like a knife through her heart. Last time he'd said anything, he'd said she'd be a great mother, but he obviously didn't believe it. It was one thing for her to think that she'd be useless, but to hear it from her brother was another. Was she that bad a person? Tears pricked her eyes. She brushed them with the back of her hand. "You're probably right."

He must have detected something in her voice, because he stopped and looked at her. "Are you okay?"

"Yes." She grabbed another sponge and attacked the side wall. Just as well Andy was there, because if he hadn't been, she probably would have lashed out at her brother.

Together, they finished preparing and painting the room in quick time. The white was clean and fresh, a blank slate for the new owners, whoever they might be, to do with as they pleased. It reminded her of a song from her past. *Create in me a clean heart, O God, and renew a right spirit within me.* She tried to push it aside, but the melody and words stayed with her long after Simon and Andy left. They'd promised to return the following day to help her shift the furniture back, so she moved the things she needed for the night into Simon's old room. Already repainted in white, the room bore no resemblance to the teenage boy's room it had once been. Mum had styled it elegantly, but it lacked character. Scented candles and glass bottles had replaced the sports trophies he was so proud of, and a large designer mirror now hung on the wall where Star Wars posters used to be.

As evening drew in, so did a sense of loneliness. Paige was tempted to call Natalie and ask if she could spend the evening with her and Adam, but after offering them her baby, she thought that might be awkward since they hadn't given her an answer yet. Instead, she flicked on the television and sat in front of it with one of the meals Mum had left for her. She didn't deserve to be looked after so well, not after all the angst she'd caused.

She channel surfed for a while, but ended up watching an action movie on Netflix. She had to do something to get that tune out of her head. She didn't want to be convicted of her sin. She was fine the way she was.

After the movie finished, she was still edgy and thought about going out, like she used to. It wasn't even ten p.m. She could try to find her Goth friends and go to a night club. Maybe hook up with a guy. She blew out a breath and flicked the television off. No, it wasn't the thing to do in her condition, as much as she'd like to. And besides, who'd want her now?

Instead, she made a hot chocolate and carried it to the bedroom. Passing the study, the sound of an incoming Skype call caught her attention. She stepped into the room and stopped suddenly. Aiden's face flashed on the screen. Her pulse accelerated. When they'd met in Fiji at their parents' wedding, she and Aiden had hit it off. She didn't understand how, because he was a real straight shooter, but her rebellious attitudes and thoughts hadn't seemed to bother him. She recalled with fondness their time sailing the small resort catamarans, swimming in the crystal blue, warm, salty water, and the leisurely walks along the soft, sandy beaches. She'd dared to dream that maybe he might feature in her future, but he returned to Texas and she to her Goth lifestyle in Sydney. She'd wanted to contact him, but a cynical inner voice had stopped her. Why would someone like him be interested in someone like her?

His face kept flashing on the screen. Her heart pounded.

Should she answer? *Could* she answer? She doubted he knew about her pregnancy. But he wouldn't judge, and she could do with someone to talk to right now. She blew out a breath, sat on Bruce's chair, and answered.

"Aiden, it's Paige. How are you?"

His face became clear and her heart beat faster. Why hadn't she called him?

He frowned, but appeared happy to see her. "Paige? I'm great. How are you?"

"Okay, I guess." She tried to present a happy face.

"Are you sure? You don't sound okay."

She bit her lip. How much should she tell him? Was she prepared to let him know how stupid and foolish she'd been? But she couldn't lie to him—he'd see through her in an instant. Besides, he'd find out eventually. She rubbed the back of her neck and winced. "I'm...I'm pregnant."

"Oh." He frowned again. "Dad didn't say anything about that last time we spoke."

"I've only just told them."

"Right." He paused, as if absorbing the news. "I gather you're not overly excited about it."

"Am I that easy to read?"

"You're not jumping for joy."

Her shoulders slumped. "No, I'm not. I won't bore you with the details. I was on my way to bed when I heard the call and decided to answer it. Your dad and Mum are away this weekend."

"You're there alone?"

She tugged a piece of hair and wrapped it around her

finger. "Yes. And I'm feeling alone, so it's good to talk with you."

He smiled. "I'm flattered, but you know you can always talk to God."

She let out a sigh. "Yes, but we're not on talking terms. You know that." She'd told him about her disappointment with God when they were in Fiji, and he'd told her then that He was there, waiting with open arms for her to come back. She'd shaken her head and said that would never happen.

"It can be easily remedied, Paige. He's still waiting for you."

She shook her head just like she had before. "How can you be so sure? I've done some really bad things. Really bad. Even if I wanted to talk to Him, I doubt He'd listen."

"Try Him. You've got nothing to lose."

Her voice wobbled. "I'd rather talk with you."

"That's flattering, but I can't give you the peace you're looking for. Only God can give you that."

She blew out a slow breath. Peace. That sounded nice.

"I'm happy to listen, though." She could see empathy in his eyes and hear the sincerity in his voice. Tears flooded her eyes. "Are you sure?"

"Yes. What do you want to talk about?"

She shrugged. "Everything."

Half an hour later, he offered to pray for her and she let him.

CHAPTER 13

When Bruce pulled the car into their driveway after their weekend away, Wendy smiled. Simon's car was there, which meant that he was. But her smile immediately slipped. "I hope nothing's wrong with Paige."

Bruce reached out and squeezed her hand. "I'm sure there's nothing to worry about. He's probably just come for a visit."

"I hope you're right."

"If we go in, we'll find out."

She laughed at the mischievous twinkle in Bruce's eye, but then grew serious. "Thank you for a lovely weekend, darling. It was perfect."

"It was. And it still is." He lifted his hand to her cheek and gently drew her face towards his until their lips brushed.

Her heart burst with love as she closed her eyes and became lost in his kiss. She finally pulled away. "We'd best go in."

"Yes, we should."

She laughed when he stole another kiss. As she opened the

car door and climbed out, her gaze was drawn to the double-pink azalea blooms that had just opened and looked spectacular. Spring was definitely here, and soon the garden would be aflourish with colour. Too bad they wouldn't be here to see it. The thought saddened her a little. She'd miss this home with all its memories, but it was time. The wheels were in motion and they planned to list the house within the next week or two.

Bruce opened the boot and lifted out their luggage. She walked ahead of him, and as she opened the door, the smell of fresh paint wafted out. "I wonder what we're going to find," she said with a mixture of anticipation and dread. Simon and Paige's tastes in colour and design were so different from hers.

"Hello. We're home," she called, looking around as they entered and walked along the hallway towards the kitchen.

Nothing. She turned and looked at Bruce. "I wonder where they are."

"Maybe they're hiding," he suggested with a wink.

She chuckled. "They're not children."

"I'll take the bags upstairs while you find them."

"Okay. Would you like a cup of tea?"

"Yes, please."

"Coming right up." Stepping into the kitchen, she stopped in her tracks and blinked. A young man stood at the sink with his back to her. Definitely not Simon. Must be his house mate. Tall with an athletic build, his muscles bulged under his white T-shirt. He must have heard her approach because he turned around.

"I'm sorry to startle you," she said.

He wiped his hands on his faded jeans and stepped towards

her, hand extended. "We were expecting you. I'm Andy, Simon's friend." His smile was engaging. Warm.

She took his hand. Shook it. Smiled. "Nice to meet you at last. So, where *is* Simon?"

"Sorting boxes in the garage."

Wendy grinned. "Oh my. I don't believe it." She walked to the kettle and filled it with water.

He leaned back against the counter. "He said you'd say that."

"Yes, well they've only been sitting there for I don't know how long."

"He's a naughty boy."

"He is. I'm making tea. Would you like one?" she asked.

"That's kind of you. Yes, I'd love one."

She smiled. "I'll make a pot. Simon might like one as well. Is Paige around?"

"I think she's taking a nap."

"That's good." Wendy frowned. "Is she okay?" As soon as she asked, she thought how strange it was to be asking this stranger about her pregnant daughter. But he was easy to talk to and she felt comfortable with him.

"Seems to be. Although she probably shouldn't have tried to paint her room on her own." He let out a small laugh.

"Absolutely not. I gather you came to help?"

"Yes. Today and yesterday."

"That's so kind of you. Thank you."

"It's not a problem."

Opening a cupboard, she lifted out her large teapot and placed five teaspoons of tea leaves into it. "What do you do, Andy?"

Leaning against the counter, he folded his arms, looking relaxed and at home. "I'm a nurse."

Wendy glanced at him again. *That's why he's so sensitive.* "Where do you work?"

"Royal Albert. Palliative Care Unit."

Her eyes widened. "Really? That must be hard."

"Yes, but it's also kind of special. We give the best care possible and I like to think we help make our patients' last days more comfortable and bearable."

"Well, I admire you. It takes a special person to do that."

He broke into an open, friendly smile. "Thank you."

The kettle boiled and Wendy poured the water into the pot. Hearing footsteps, she turned around. Bruce appeared in the doorway and she held her hand out to him. "Bruce, this is Simon's house mate, Andy."

The two men shook hands and started chatting while Wendy finished making the tea. She also quickly prepared a simple share platter of crackers, cheese and dip. "Shall we have this on the deck?" she asked Bruce.

"Sure. Can I carry something?"

She handed him the teapot and the platter.

"I'll fetch Simon," Andy said.

She smiled gratefully and thanked him. When he disappeared downstairs, she followed Bruce outside with a tray of mugs she set on the table. "He's such a nice young man. A palliative care nurse at the Royal Albert." Her voice carried an element of pride, although she didn't know why. He was only Simon's house mate.

"That's different," Bruce replied.

"Yes, it is." She pulled out a chair and as she sat beside him, her gaze was drawn to the harbour below. Although Avoca was lovely, this was home, and the view was stunning. A couple of yachts sailed by at a leisurely pace, silhouetted in the late afternoon sunshine, and in the distance, the Manly ferry chugged across the harbour. It was going to be difficult to leave.

Simon, appearing with Andy, leaned over and kissed her cheek. "Hey Mum. How was your weekend?"

"Great, thank you. I hear you're finally sorting your boxes."

He chuckled. "Sorry it's taken so long."

"It's okay. The talk of moving obviously made a difference."

"Yes." He motioned for Andy to sit, and then sat beside him. "And Paige decided to paint her room."

"Yes, so Andy told me."

"Silly girl. Thought she could do it on her own."

"I'm glad you came to her rescue. Both of you." She smiled first at Simon and then at Andy.

"I think it wore her out. She's been asleep since lunch."

"I'll check on her in a minute. Before I do, shall I pour?"

"Allow me." Andy stood and picked up the teapot.

Wendy smiled gratefully.

As Andy poured, she thought again what a nice young man he was and how lovely it would be if he and Paige got together. She deserved someone caring like Andy after all the no-hopers she'd dated.

Moments later, after the tea had been poured and the mugs distributed, Paige joined them. Her hair, draped over her shoulders, was speckled with white. Wendy felt relieved. She hadn't dared ask Andy what colour she'd painted her room, but white was good.

Wendy held out her hand and smiled. "Hello sweetheart. Did you have a good sleep?"

Paige nodded. Yawned. Stretched her neck. "How was your weekend?" She squeezed Wendy's hand and then sat opposite, accepting a mug of tea from Andy with a nod of thanks.

"Lovely, thank you, but it's nice to be home. Especially with you all here. We just need Natalie and Adam to turn up now. Maybe we should invite them over."

"I think they had other plans," Paige said quickly.

Wendy frowned. Was something going on that she didn't know about? "Oh, well. Another time." She sipped her tea and while Bruce, Andy and Simon chatted, she asked Paige how she was feeling.

"Tired. Fat. Uncomfortable."

"The joys of pregnancy." Wendy chuckled, recalling her own. Paige was hardly fat, but considering how thin she normally was, any bump would seem like a mountain to her. "Has the baby been active?"

Nodding, Paige placed her hands on her tummy. She looked forlorn, lost, confused. Her eyes moistened.

Shifting closer, Wendy slipped her arm around Paige's shoulder. "It's okay, sweetheart."

Paige sniffed and wrapped her hands around her mug.

Wendy's heart went out to her. Reluctant to talk about Paige's pregnancy in front of Andy for fear of embarrassing her, Wendy offered her the cheese platter and asked about the bedroom. "I'm looking forward to seeing it."

Paige nodded and nibbled a cracker.

"I'm glad you asked for help." Wendy's gaze shifted to Andy. He and Bruce were engaged in a conversation about health care, and she gathered from what he was saying that he may have undertaken some training in the States. "He seems like a nice young man. It was good of him to come," she said quietly.

"Don't try to match make me, Mum. He's g…good with people, but he's spoken for."

Wendy immediately felt deflated. "So, he has a girlfriend. I wish Simon would find one."

"He's happy enough, Mum. Leave him alone."

Suitably told off, Wendy chastised herself once again for meddling in her children's lives. She'd been determined not to control what they did or influence their life choices unless they asked for her input, which they rarely did. She truly cared about them and wanted to see them happy, but they were adults and had their own lives to live. And like Paige said, Simon *did* seem happy. She still disliked how he kept things to himself, but he was a good person, and he'd do anything to help his sister. Maybe one day he'd find a girl to settle down with, but in the meantime, he seemed content on his own.

Darkness slowly crept in. Lights flickered on the other side of the harbour making it look like fairy land. This too, she would miss when they lived on acreage. Taking a deep breath of fresh air, she rubbed her arms.

"Getting cold, my darling?" Bruce slipped his arm around her and pulled her close.

She nodded, snuggling closer. "We should go in, but I don't want to." The weekend had been perfect, but she had work in the morning and needed to prepare.

Andy stood and pushed his chair back. "As nice as this is, it's time we went. Thank you for your hospitality." He held his hand out to Bruce. "It's been lovely meeting you."

"You're welcome, son. Come back any time." Bruce stood and shook his hand.

"Thank you." He then turned to Wendy and held his hand out, smiling. "Thanks for the tea."

"And thank *you* for helping." She ignored his hand and gave him a hug.

"It was a pleasure." Finally, he turned to Paige and gave her a hug. "Look after yourself and that baby."

"I'll try to."

Simon bid everyone goodbye and carried the teapot and empty platter to the kitchen on his way out. "In case you're wondering, we'll come back with Andy's pickup tomorrow after work to collect the boxes."

"I appreciate that. And thanks for your help." Pulling him close, Wendy gave him a big hug.

"You're welcome. I hope you can help Paige sort herself out. She's so mixed up and has no idea what she wants," he whispered into her ear.

"I know. I'll do my best." She glanced at Paige and prayed for wisdom.

CHAPTER 14

*T*wo weeks later, a 'For Sale' sign went up in front of the house and Wendy and Bruce began searching for their new home in earnest. After inspecting many and praying a lot, they fell in love with a country estate five kilometres west of Castle Hill. Elevated, with views to the Blue Mountains, the property offered a large two-level residence, a swimming pool surrounded by tropical palms, a huge shed complete with equipment, and most importantly of all, a horse corral and five horses. Bruce was ecstatic, Wendy, slightly anxious. "It's so big," she said to him during their third inspection.

He chuckled and wrapped her in a bear hug. "You don't know what big is, darlin'."

She guessed he was right. Compared to his ranch in Texas, this was miniscule, but after the small piece of land perched on the side of a hill in Cremorne that had been her home for years, it seemed gigantic. "How do we look after it?" Thoughts of replacing her job with constant cleaning and yardwork didn't thrill her. Not that she shied away from work, but she didn't want it to be all consuming.

"We can get a cleaner and someone to help outside. Don't worry about it, sweetheart."

"As long as you're sure."

"I am." He kissed the top of her head. "Shall we put in an offer?"

She took a deep breath. "Okay." Her voice was tiny.

Their offer was accepted, but was dependent on the sale of the Cremorne house. They didn't have long to wait. A young couple inspected it and placed an offer the following day, which they accepted. Three weeks later, they moved. All the family, plus Andy, as well as Wendy's friend, Robyn, came to help.

After a full day of unpacking, the house began to resemble home. The new furniture they'd ordered arrived and looked great. Paige had wanted to keep her furniture, as well as the living room furniture from the Cremorne house, to put in her wing of the house. Wendy could understand that. Although only timber and fabric, the furniture held a connection to the past. The past she knew Paige still clung to, although, to Wendy's relief, she seemed to be slowly letting go of.

Robyn offered to help Paige settle into her wing. After hearing they'd bumped into each other and chatted about Paige's situation, Wendy thought it a perfect idea. Paige was still flip-flopping, although she'd formally offered the baby to Natalie and Adam. They'd told her that after praying about it and discussing it, they would love to adopt the baby girl, but would understand if she changed her mind, either before she was born, or even soon after. Paige said that didn't help her in the slightest. She would have preferred a definite answer so the decision was taken from her, and she started to wish she'd gone through the normal adoption channels. Wendy prayed that Robyn might help her with her deliberations, having been through it herself.

Andy and Simon worked together like well-oiled machines as they shifted furniture around, trying it in different spots until Wendy was happy with the positioning of everything. At one stage, she asked Andy where his girlfriend was. He gave her a blank look, and then told her he didn't have one. She frowned, but shrugged it off, assuming they must have broken up recently or that Paige had gotten it wrong.

They finished the day off with a take-out meal from the local Indian restaurant. Later, once everyone had gone, Wendy and Bruce sat outside drinking tea, admiring the star-studded sky. The silence was deafening. No cars, buses or ferries rushing by, just the occasional sound of a horse neighing or a dog barking.

Bruce held her hand, gently rubbing his thumb over her skin. "Are you happy, darlin'?"

"Yes. Exhausted, but happy. It's our brand new beginning, and I already love it."

He lifted her hand to his mouth and pressed his lips softly against it. "Thank you."

"For what?"

"For giving up your home to move here."

"Oh, sweetheart. It wasn't hard in the end. A house is only

bricks and mortar, after all. It's the people who live there that make it a home. And my home is wherever you are."

"You'd best stop it or you might see a grown man brought to tears. I still find it hard to believe that we found each other, but I'm so glad we did."

"And so am I. And it's me who should be thanking you for choosing to live here."

"It was an easy choice. Although I'm looking forward to seeing my family at Christmas."

"I know you are."

"Yes, and now that we have a home, we can cancel that rental booking."

Wendy's shoulders fell. "I was looking forward to a holiday at the beach. How about we keep it for just one week instead of the three? I'm sure the kids will enjoy it."

"Sounds like a good option. The week after Christmas?"

"Perfect. We just have to pray that Paige's baby doesn't come while we're away."

"It'll come when it's ready, and whenever it does will be fine."

"Yes, I know. I feel so much for Natalie and Adam at the moment. They don't know if they're going to become parents or not. They've been amazing about the whole situation. I don't know if I could have been so accommodating." She twiddled with a loose thread on his shirt.

"They're an amazing couple. I'm sure God will bless them, one way or the other."

"I'm sure He will. It's just a guessing game as to which way." Wendy stifled a yawn. "I think I need to go to bed."

"I agree. We're getting too old for all of this."

"Speak for yourself." She slapped him playfully on the chest and laughed.

He grabbed her hand, then wrapped his other arm around her. "But I'm not too old for this." His blue eyes twinkled with mischief before his mouth covered hers hungrily, the strong hardness of his lips sending the pit of her stomach into a wild swirl and her pulse skittering. She pushed him away gently. "I think we really do need to go to bed."

He laughed and stood, then helped her up. Encircling her with one arm, he gazed into her eyes and cupped her cheek with his other hand. "Our first night in our new home." He smiled as he lowered his mouth again, this time, kissing her slowly but passionately.

PAIGE FLOPPED onto her bed and stared at the ceiling. How would she survive? This place was so far from anywhere. Why had she agreed to come here? As soon as she had the baby, she'd move back to the city, but she'd have to survive until then —she had no option.

But what if she kept it?

She'd need to stay longer as she couldn't look after it on her own, at least to start with. The thought scared her, but with every kick, she was coming to care for the baby growing inside her and the thought of giving her up, even to Natalie and Adam, filled her with sadness. But could she be a good mother? That was the question that haunted her. It wasn't enough to want the baby. She had to commit her whole life to it. Well, at least the next twenty years. That was a long time. And it would restrict what she did. But did that matter? She hadn't done anything much with her life until now anyway.

She sighed heavily and rolled over. As she did, the baby moved. Six weeks to decide. Six weeks to survive. She struggled to fall asleep. The bed was hers, but the room was strange. Clinical. Quiet. She got up and turned the television on but all she could get were the local channels. The cable wasn't connected yet.

Frustrated, she turned the television off and stepped outside. Her eyes popped open. The stars were so bright she initially thought they were street lights until she realised they were too high. The night air was cool on her cheek but it felt nice. Refreshing. Pulling her robe tighter, she sat on the edge of a sandstone wall and looked up. Rarely venturing from the city, she'd hadn't seen a night sky like this since she was a small child when Dad had taken her, Simon, and Natalie camping. She remembered lying on her back and listening in awe as Dad pointed out the stars and constellations. He knew so many of them. She struggled to remember one. But as she concentrated, she thought she might have found the Southern Cross. Dad would be proud.

He'd also said that what they could see was just a teensy portion of the universe. Their view was so small, just like their view of God. God was so much bigger, so much greater than anyone could ever imagine. He was eternal. He had no beginning and no end. It was more than she could comprehend, then, or now. But as she gazed into the sky, something inside her shifted, and it wasn't the baby. She used to believe in a God who loved her. Maybe He still did. *But did she still believe?* She'd closed her mind and heart to Him, but many had told her that He hadn't abandoned her. She'd been the one who'd walked away, not Him. She just had to reach out and seek Him. She knew she had to stop blaming Him for Dad's death. People died all the time. She knew that. She'd been angry. Bitter. Disappointed. But she'd been the one who'd suffered. She knew that when Jesus died on the cross and rose again, he won the victory over death, not just for Himself, but for all who believed in Him and chose to live their lives for Him. Dad believed, but she'd walked away when he died. It was one thing knowing it in your head, but knowing it in your heart was what mattered.

Renewed anguish filled her. She missed him so much. Tears slowly found their way down her cheeks.

He's with Me, my child.

She closed her eyes. God was talking to her, like He had been all along. Why had she been so stubborn for so long?

"God, I'm sorry. I truly am. Please forgive me. I'm sorry for blaming You for taking Dad." She sniffed. "Look after him. Tell him I love him." She wiped her eyes and sat quietly. Breathing in the cool, fresh air she opened her heart anew to God, the author and creator of the universe, who loved her so much that He sent His only Son to earth so that she might have new life filled with hope and purpose. "Lord God, I give You my life anew. Please guide me and lead me. And bless this dear little baby. I don't deserve her, but please help me to love and care for her and to be a good mother. I'm so scared, but I know You'll be with me, as will Mum and Bruce, and the rest of my family. Please help Natalie and Adam to conceive their own baby and to not be sad when I tell them. Thank You for their understanding."

Soon after, she walked back inside and this time, fell asleep easily. When she awoke in the morning, it took a few moments to recall what had happened, but then it came back. She'd let go of the pain and anguish, and now she was free.

endy noticed the change in Paige as soon as she walked into the kitchen the following morning. It wasn't so much her appearance that was different, but her demeanour. Since Greg's passing, Paige had worn a perpetual scowl, especially in the mornings, so when she entered with a truly warm smile and gave Wendy a hug, Wendy knew that something life changing had happened.

"I'm sorry for everything, Mum." Paige's voice hitched and she began to sob.

Wendy pulled her close and blinked back tears of her own. "It's okay, sweetheart. I love you, you know that."

Sniffing, Paige nodded. "I'm going to keep the baby." Her voice was quiet, soft.

Warmth flooded Wendy's heart. For some time, she'd sensed that Paige had been softening towards the baby, but she hadn't expected her to decide until she delivered. "You'll be a great mother, darling. And we'll help as much as we can."

Paige sniffed again and wiped her nose with a tissue she pulled from her pocket. "Thank you." She remained silent for several moments before she spoke again. "You might be pleased to know that I'm back on talking terms with God."

Wendy's eyes widened and she pulled Paige close and hugged her again. "Oh Paige, you don't know how happy that makes me." Wendy's heart sang with joy. It was such an answer to prayer. She'd often wavered in her faith, despairing over Paige's bitterness and anger towards God, but when she was young, Paige had displayed a genuine love for God, and deep down, Wendy had known that one day she'd let go of her anger and reach out to Him. And now, she had. What a truly wonderful day!

"I don't know why it took me so long. I guess I'm just stubborn."

Wendy laughed. "I guess you are! Let me make a cup of tea and we can sit and chat."

"I'd like that. Can I help?"

Wendy smiled to herself. Her girl was back. "It's okay, sweetheart. Sit down and I'll get it. How are you feeling?"

"Good." Paige pulled out a chair and sat at the large wooden table. "I'm not looking forward to telling Natalie."

"She'll be okay. I think deep down she knew you'd decide to keep your baby."

"Really?"

"Yes. She knows you better than you think."

"That makes me feel not quite so bad. I'm still not ready to be a mother, but I don't think I could give the baby up."

"You'll be fine, sweetie. Your maternal instincts will kick in, and I'll help, if you want me to." Wendy set a mug of tea in front of her. "Would you like some toast?"

"Yes, please."

"We're going to try out a new church today. Would you like to come with us?"

Paige rubbed her tummy. "What will people think?"

"Don't worry about that. If they're true Christians, they won't judge. If they do, we'll find another church."

"Okay, then. I guess I'll come."

Wendy's heart almost burst at the seams. Having Paige attend church with them was more than she could ever have wished or prayed for.

PAIGE WALKED between Wendy and Bruce as they approached the entrance of the Hills Christian Church that morning. Positioned in the middle of the village, the traditional building stood out amongst the array of trendy craft shops and cafés that lined the stretch of road on either side. It seemed that Sunday morning was a popular time for people to eat out and browse the shops, but a good number were also headed for church.

Paige steeled herself for stony stares and raised brows, but was pleasantly surprised when they were greeted with smiling faces and welcoming handshakes. It had been many years since she'd been in church. She used to love singing and worship, and now, as the band played one of her favourite worship songs, her spirit quickened and she wondered why she'd stopped going.

Pausing, she motioned for Bruce to go ahead and followed him and Mum into a row of seats towards the back. Although the exterior of the building was traditional with a steeple and a cross, the interior had been modified to fit a band, complete with piano, two guitarists, a full drum kit and drummer, and three singers at the front. The church filled up quickly, and as the congregation joined in worship, Paige felt that she'd come home.

The sermon given by the head pastor, John Hodges, a tall, middle-aged man with short ginger hair, immediately grabbed her attention. Entitled *'Why doesn't God always answer our prayers?',* Paige's ears pricked as soon as he began.

"How long are we supposed to keep praying if God continues to ignore us? In Psalm 84:11 the Psalmist writes, 'No good thing will God withhold from those who walk uprightly.' That seems simple enough, but God's idea of a 'good thing' often differs from ours.

"You might be praying for a husband, or a job you've been hoping for, or even to win the lottery. Why wouldn't God give you any or all of these? They're all good things. But God might think they're not right for you and He might have other plans. Just because something makes us happy doesn't mean it's the right thing for us, *eternally.* And that's what's most important— God has our *eternal* interests in mind, not necessarily our earthly best. Being comfortable and getting what we want isn't always a good thing.

"We need to trust that God, our Heavenly Father, truly knows what's best for us. While we might be heartbroken at His 'no', He may very well be saving us from a bigger heartache down the road.

"God may also be waiting for us to be obedient. The verse says 'no good thing will He withhold from those who walk *uprightly.*' The question also is, are we walking uprightly? Are we not only obedient, but fully surrendered to Him? If not, God might be holding out in acknowledging our prayers to get us back into line with His will and purposes.

"God has three answers to our prayers. Yes, no, and wait. Because He can see what's eternally best for us and He can also see what our future holds, we need to trust His judgement. We shouldn't second-guess Him. His timing is always better than ours. If we're walking uprightly and what we're praying for is truly a good thing, then, according to the psalm, God isn't ignoring us. It just isn't the right time.

"And lastly, because God is good and knows what's eternally best for us, He sometimes says 'no' because He has something better in store. Something we haven't even thought to ask for. Ephesians 3:20 says that 'He can do immeasurably more than all we can ask or imagine.' Trust His timing. Trust His 'no'. And trust His idea of what's best for you, *eternally.* He truly is a good Father. His ways are higher than ours and He knows what's best for us."

Pausing, the pastor cast his gaze around the congregation. "Can you trust Him, regardless of His answer to your prayers?"

Paige brushed tears from her eyes. All those years of blaming God for not answering hers. She saw now that her prayers were selfish. She wanted Dad to be there for *her.* What daughter wouldn't? But she had to trust Him and believe that He had something better in store for Dad, and for her, just like everyone had been telling her.

As the pastor ended, he asked any who wanted prayer to

come forward. Paige's heart beat faster. She had to go. She had to respond. It was like scales had been removed from not only her eyes, but from her heart, and all of a sudden she wanted nothing else but to be in His presence. She needed Him. Her Father. Her eternal, loving and good Father. She stood and slowly waddled forward, tears streaming down her cheeks. Joining several others, she kneeled down and bowed her head as the Holy Spirit ministered to her. She felt a hand on her head and then heard the voice of the pastor as he prayed for her.

Standing a short while later, she returned to her seat and smiled at Mum and Bruce. Mum reached past him and hugged her. "God bless you, sweetheart. You've made my heart glad." She had tears in her eyes and seemed overwhelmed.

"Thank you. And I'm sorry for all I've put you through," Paige replied, sniffing.

"It's in the past now, sweetheart. Let's move on."

She nodded. "Thank you."

"You're welcome, sweetie." Mum hugged her again and then released her as the final hymn began.

Be still, my soul, The Lord is on thy side.
Bear patiently, the cross of grief or pain.
Leave to thy God, to order and provide.
In every change, He faithful will remain.
Be still, my soul, Thy best Thy heavenly Friend.
Through thorny ways, leads to a joyful end.

Paige would have preferred to go directly home. Emotionally tired, she could think of nothing better than curling up on her bed and taking a nap, even though it was still morning. But being new, and most likely because of her expectant state and response to the sermon, she, Mum and Bruce had drawn the attention of their fellow worshippers. One after the after, members of the congregation introduced themselves to the trio and invited them to stay for coffee. Mum, aware of her need for rest, whispered in her ear that it would be rude not to, but that they'd only stay for a short time.

Paige reluctantly agreed and followed them into the adjoining hall where people had already gathered in groups and were drinking coffee and chatting. Mostly older people. Well dressed, well-to-do. Paige was used to this. Their church in Sydney was in an affluent area, but all of a sudden she felt out of place. Would any of these people, as kindly and friendly as they were, know what it's like to sleep rough? To be homeless? To be pregnant and alone? Probably not. She wouldn't judge them because of that. It wasn't their fault, but she suddenly had an idea. She'd finish her Uni course but add a major in Social Work and when she finished, she'd work among the homeless. She'd do something worthwhile with her life. But then she stopped. She hadn't prayed about it. Was this what God wanted for her, or was she just racing ahead? She sighed. *Okay, God, I'll pray about it. Guide me and lead me. If this is what You want, I'm willing. If it's not, this time I'll listen, I promise.*

Finally arriving home, Paige took a nap, falling asleep the instant her head hit the pillow.

CHAPTER 16

Standing in the garage of their new home with Bruce, Wendy surveyed the mountain of boxes and sighed. "Can we leave them until tomorrow?"

"I don't see why not. There's no real hurry, and besides, everything we truly need was unpacked yesterday. And I think I might like a little time alone with my wife." He slipped his arms around her from behind and nuzzled her neck.

She laughed. "Bruce! It's the middle of the day. And it's Sunday."

"Does that matter?"

"Yes! Paige could wake up at any minute."

"Okay. You win. Come and walk with me, then. I want to explore the property." He released her and took her hand. She had no option but to follow.

With the summer sun beating down, she grabbed a hat on the way out and put it on. Stepping outside, the mountains in the distance, covered in a simmering heat haze, beckoned to her. "Do you think we can take a drive up there one day soon?"

"Of course." He turned and looked at her as they walked along the gravel path towards the horse paddock. "I do hope you'll be happy out here, darlin'. I'll have to teach you to ride."

She shook her head. "I don't think that will happen any time soon." She grew serious. "But I'd love to watch you. You know, I've never seen you on a horse."

"It's about time that changed, then. I've already decided which is my favorite."

"Let me guess."

"Go on."

They'd reached the fence and all but one of the five horses grazed lazily in the paddock. The other, a black stallion, pranced over to them when Bruce whistled.

"I think it's obvious, don't you?"

"Kinda." He smiled. "Prince. That's what the previous owners called him. I think it's an apt name."

"What are you going to do with them?" she asked. Bruce had told her he had plans, but hadn't shared them with her.

"I'm thinking we'll run a learn-to-ride school, but any money we make will go straight to a charity organisation. We don't need it, but others do."

A lump caught in Wendy's throat. Bruce was such a generous man. "That's a lovely plan. Now, let me see you ride."

"Now? He's not saddled."

"Can't you ride bare-back?"

"Yes, but I wouldn't risk injury on a horse I don't know."

"Why don't you saddle him and I'll make a pot of tea and watch while you ride."

"I've got a better idea. I'll take you for a ride."

Her jaw dropped. "On him?"

"No." He laughed. "You can ride the mare."

Wendy shifted her gaze to the paddock. All the horses looked intimidating. "I don't know. I'd probably fall off."

"No, you won't. I'll help you."

She sighed and ran her hand across her cheek. "I guess I can give it a go."

"Marvellous. I'll saddle up both horses while you get ready."

"What should I wear?"

"Jeans and closed-toe shoes."

"I don't have any jeans. You know that."

"Slacks, then. We'll need to get you some jeans next time we go shopping."

"Not likely. I've never been a jeans type of girl."

"We'll see about that." Winking, he scaled the fence as if he were still a man of twenty, not sixty plus, and swaggered towards the mare that stood sedate. It let Bruce approach without flinching or running, so perhaps it *was* a calm horse.

"I'll go and get ready," she called out.

Turning, he tipped his hat and replied, "See you soon."

Wendy hurried back to the house and changed into a pair of light blue slacks. Bruce would never get her into jeans, even if they were more practical. She just wasn't a jeans person. She sat on the bed and put on her joggers. Standing, she glanced in the mirror and grimaced. It wasn't a great look. Jeans might actually be better. Maybe she would buy some if she was going to start riding. But she'd see how this ride went first.

Passing Paige's wing, she was tempted to check on her. She placed her hand on the door handle but then paused. No, she'd let her sleep. She still couldn't believe the change in her daughter. It was nothing short of a miracle. A real answer to prayer. Now, all God had to do was work on Simon. She sighed as she let go of the handle and continued on. Something wasn't quite right with Simon, but she couldn't put her finger on it. He and Andy had been a great help yesterday, but she'd chatted more with Andy than with her own son, who seemed to be keeping something close to his chest. If only he'd talk with her more. Next time he came over, she'd press him a little. Maybe he was sick and didn't want to worry her. That wouldn't surprise her, but she prayed that wasn't the case.

After grabbing a bottle of water from the fridge, she headed back outside and stopped. Could she actually go through with this? Living in the city all her life, she'd had little to do with animals other than cats and dogs. She was way too old to start riding horses. *Listen to yourself, Wendy McCarthy. Stop it and just enjoy the experience.* She laughed. Okay...but if I fall off... *You won't fall off. Bruce will be holding you.*

She walked to the paddock to find him talking to the mare like she was his best friend. Wendy's heart melted. He looked so at home, so content and happy. He turned and waved her over. "She's ready. Come on, darling. Put this helmet on and then I'll help you up."

Wendy shook her head and chuckled as she walked towards him, taking the helmet from him. "I hope you're strong."

"Are you doubting my capabilities?"

"No. But I'm not the lightest of persons."

"I'm not going to hoist you onto her." He grinned.

"You're not? How do I get up?"

"You're going to stand on this mounting block and then put your foot in the stirrup. I'll help if needed."

"I hope the horse will be able to handle me."

"She's a strong old thing. She'll be fine."

"As long as you're sure." Wendy steeled herself and stepped onto the mounting block. The horse, not quite so intimidating from this height, turned her head and studied her. Wendy laughed. "I think she's sizing me up!"

"You're probably right. But I think the two of you will get on just fine."

"What are you saying?" Wendy raised a brow.

"Nothing, my love." He winked at her. "Now, hold onto the reins." He passed them into her hand. "Put your left foot into the stirrup."

She did as instructed, but then, when he told her to lift her right leg over the horse, she couldn't do it. "I think I need to go back to the gym."

"Give it another try. I'll help."

Sighing, she bit her lip and concentrated. Bruce had interlaced his fingers and told her to rest her knee in the support he'd made. "It will give leverage, and I'll push."

"Good luck with that!" She laughed nervously before refocusing. "Okay, I can do this."

"I believe in you."

She met his gaze and almost hit him. He was having fun at her expense. "I was going to say 'thank you', but I don't think I will."

"I'm sorry, Wendy, I shouldn't be making fun of you."

"No, you shouldn't. Not if you want me to go riding."

"Okay. I'll behave."

"Good." She took a deep breath and focused. She could do this. How hard was it to lift a leg over a horse? If only she hadn't given up her gym membership. The horse, whose name was Marcy, turned her head again, almost as if to say, 'what are you doing?'

Wendy patted her. "Be patient with me, old girl. I haven't done this before." Wendy could have sworn that the horse nodded. She shook her head and patted her again. "Okay. Here I go." She pressed her knee into Bruce's interlaced fingers and hefted her right leg over Marcy's back. In the process, she overbalanced and her head landed on Marcy's neck. She laughed and wrapped her arms around the horse. "I'm sorry. I hope I'm not too heavy for you." She pushed herself up and then smiled at Bruce. "I made it."

"You certainly did. I'll make a rider of you yet."

"Don't make fun of me."

"I'm not. I'm proud of you."

She chuckled. "If only the kids could see me."

"I'll call them if you'd like."

"Don't you dare!"

"I was joking. Okay, how do you feel?"

She shifted in the saddle. "Strange. Uncomfortable."

"I'll adjust the stirrups. They're a bit too high."

"Okay. Maybe that's the problem."

She sat patiently while he made the adjustments.

"How's that?"

"Better."

"Good. Before we head off for an actual ride, we'll do a short round of the upper paddock so you can get a feel for it. I'll hold the rope and lead you."

"Okay. As long as she doesn't take off."

"She won't. She's as steady as they come."

"She'd better be."

He laughed. "Okay, here we go. Sit tall but relaxed, hold the reins loosely, and sit square in the saddle."

"Relax? How can I do that?"

"Breathe slowly. You'll be fine. You look good." He winked again.

"You're loving this, aren't you?"

"And if I am?"

She shrugged. "I guess it's okay."

"Right, away we go."

Wendy tried to remember his instructions as Marcy began walking. She felt awfully awkward, as if she could topple off at any moment. How could anyone possibly stay on if the horse went any faster?

"Try to relax. It's supposed to be enjoyable." Bruce walked slightly ahead of the horse and looked back at her.

"I'm trying."

"I know you are. You're doing well."

When they reached the end of the paddock, he showed her how to pull gently on the reins to get Marcy to stop. Then he showed her how to make her turn. When they returned to the shed, he asked if she felt confident enough to take a short ride.

"Wouldn't you rather go on your own? I'll only slow you down."

"I can't think of anything I'd rather be doing. A Sunday afternoon ride with my beautiful wife—what more could a man wish for?"

"You're too smooth, Mr. McCarthy." But she was joking.

She loved his way of making her feel special. It warmed her heart so, and made her ever so grateful for their unexpected romance.

"I'll take that as a yes. I'll untie Prince and then we'll be off."

"Are you just going to leave me? What if she takes off?"

"She won't, but I'll tie her up anyway."

"Good. I wouldn't have any idea what to do if she suddenly took off. I'd probably fall."

"We don't want that to happen." He took Marcy's lead rope and secured it to the rail, untied Prince, and mounted the tall, black, athletic looking horse, making it look so easy. Wendy would have been disappointed if he hadn't. He then untied Marcy and they were off.

CHAPTER 17

When Paige woke, her gaze travelled around the room. Where was she? The bed was hers, but the room was unfamiliar. And then it came back. They'd moved house, and this was her new bedroom. She tried to sit but fell back on the bed. Her head was dizzy, her body clammy, and her hands and feet were swollen like over-blown balloons. She'd overdone it yesterday and now was paying the price. She didn't feel good at all. Placing a hand on her forehead, her eyes drooped and she fell into a fitful sleep.

Sometime later, searing pain from just under her ribs woke her again. Groaning, she grabbed her stomach and stumbled to the bathroom. After vomiting into the toilet bowl, the thought crossed her mind that maybe she had food poisoning. Whatever it was, she felt like death.

Managing to stand at the basin, she splashed water over her face, but pain hit again. Surely, she wasn't in labour. It was too early. But something was wrong. Holding her stomach, she made her way out of the bathroom and into the main part of the house. Mum and Bruce weren't around, but the house was so big they could be anywhere.

She couldn't keep walking. Collapsing onto the couch, she pulled her phone from her pocket and dialed Mum's number. She groaned when it rang in the kitchen. Wherever Mum was, she'd gone out without her phone. She then tried Bruce's. It went straight to voice mail. She didn't leave a message. She had to get help from someone. *Natalie?* No. She lived too far away now. *Simon? Maybe. Yes...Andy was a nurse. He'd know what to do.* She quickly dialed Simon's number. He answered on the second ring.

"Paige. What are you up to?"

"I'm...I'm not feeling good."

"What's wrong?" She could hear the panic in his voice.

"I don't know. Food poisoning or...or I might be in labour."

"But it's too soon. Where's Mum?"

"I don't know. She's not here and she didn't take her phone. Bruce isn't answering either."

"I'll call an ambulance."

"Don't do that. It's not that bad."

"Are you sure?"

"I don't know. I don't know what's wrong." She began to sob.

"We'll come over. We can be there in ten minutes."

"That would be great. Thank you."

"No problem. I'll grab Andy and we'll get going. Call if you get worse."

"I will."

Paige closed her eyes and tried to ignore the dizziness and

pain. The thought flashed across her mind that something might be wrong with the baby. After all she'd been through, that wouldn't be fair. She prayed silently, pleading with God to keep it safe. She tried not to think about her last request from God when she'd asked Him to save her dad from dying. Could she stay true to her renewed commitment, or would she falter at the first hurdle? Could she trust God, regardless? Had it just been this morning she'd been in church and walked forward? How could her faith be tested so soon? She bit her lip as pain gripped her again. It didn't feel like a contraction, but then, since she'd never had one before, she didn't know what to expect.

The pain dissipated. Minutes passed. She had to stay calm. Nothing bad was going to happen. Simon and Andy were on their way. Then she heard voices. And then the door. "Mum..." Her voice was raspy. Ragged.

No response.

She called out again, this time louder. Moments later, Mum was at her side and Paige burst into tears.

"Sweetheart, what's the matter?" Mum soothed her forehead with her hand.

"I feel sick, and I think the baby might be coming." She sobbed and found it hard to control her breathing.

"What makes you think that?"

"I'm in pain."

"Whereabouts, sweetheart?"

Paige placed her hands on her upper abdomen. "Here."

"I don't think it's labour. But I think we need to get you to the hospital. You're swollen like a balloon."

"I think I overdid it yesterday."

"Maybe. Although I didn't think so."

"I called Simon and Andy. They're on their way." She could hardly speak.

"Why didn't you call me?" Mum frowned and felt around in her pocket.

"You left your phone in the kitchen." Paige struggled to sit.

"Oh. I'm sorry."

"And Bruce's went straight to voice mail."

"He must have been talking to Aiden when you called."

Despite her pain, Paige's ears pricked up at the mention of his name.

"Have you had anything to eat or drink?" Mum felt her forehead again.

"No."

"That's probably for the best." Her voice trailed away.

"Why?" Paige frowned.

Mum hesitated and blew out a breath. "Just in case..."

"In case what?" Paige's gaze narrowed.

Squeezing her hand, Mum replied quietly. "In case the baby needs to be delivered."

Tears clouded Paige's vision. "Today? You mean I could have the baby today?"

"It's possible, sweetheart. Let's get you to the hospital and see what they say."

"But Simon and Andy are coming here."

"It's okay. I'll call and let them know." She looked up. "It's too late, I just heard a car."

Paige wriggled to get more comfortable.

"I don't think you should move, sweetheart."

She began hyperventilating. "Am I going to be okay?"

"Yes, I'm sure you'll be fine. Take some slow breaths. That's the way."

Simon and Andy appeared. Bruce stood behind them.

Andy approached, sat beside her, and quickly wrapped a blood pressure monitoring cuff around her arm. "I'm going to check your blood pressure, Paige." He placed the stethoscope on her arm and then pumped air into the cuff. Paige caught the glance between him and her mother. Something was definitely wrong. "What's the matter?"

Mum squeezed her hand. Andy cleared his throat. "Your blood pressure's sky high. You need to get to the hospital straight away."

"Am I going to die?"

"Not if we can help it. Stay calm. We'll call for an ambulance."

"Do we have time?" Mum asked, sounding alarmed. "We could probably get her to the hospital before they even get here."

Andy shook his head. "She's better off in an ambulance. We'll tell them it's an emergency."

How she wished she hadn't heard that. Tears spilled down her cheeks.

"I'll call now," he said, pulling out his phone. He walked away, out of her hearing.

Paige's head swam. She felt nauseous. "I'm going to be sick." She leaned to the side and heaved the contents of her stomach into an empty fruit bowl Mum had quickly grabbed off the coffee table and thrust under her face. This was a nightmare. She'd never felt so sick in all her life. What was happening?

Bruce took the filled bowl away. Mum thanked him and asked

him to grab a damp washcloth. When he returned with one, she wiped Paige's face. "There, sweetheart. I hope that feels better."

"It does. Thank you."

"You're welcome. Now, lie back down."

Paige complied, but grabbed Mum's hand. "What's happening? Be honest, please."

Her mother drew a slow breath. "It looks like pre-eclampsia to me, but we'll need to get that confirmed."

Paige's eyes shot open. "People die from that, don't they?"

Mum squeezed her hand. "Try not to worry. The ambulance will be here soon."

Paige's mind whirled as she tried to remember what she'd heard about the condition. The thing that stuck in her mind was that the only cure was to deliver the baby. She was only thirty-four weeks, and the baby was still small. It was too early. The doctor had wanted her to carry it beyond full-term if possible, and definitely not have it early. She began panting and grew hot and clammy again.

Do you trust Me? She blinked. Tried to slow her breaths. It wasn't fair. *Why are You testing me now? Why don't You let me go full-term? You can fix this if You want.*

There you go again. Questioning Me again.

Paige let out a huge sigh. Yes, she was doing it again. Was she that slow of a learner? *I'm sorry. I **will** trust You. I'm sorry for panicking.*

"The ambulance will be here in five minutes," Andy said, striding into the room. "How's she doing?"

"Much the same," Mum said.

Paige closed her eyes. If she was going to trust, she needed to stay calm. Let them do their jobs. Let them look after her. Care for her.

Everything that happened after that was a blur. The ambulance came. A siren wailed. Lights flashed. She was transferred to a gurney and rushed into Emergency, where they hooked her up to machines that beeped and flashed. Doctors and nurses hovered around her. She heard the word 'emergency caesarian', and the next thing she knew, she was in the operating theatre.

"We're going to put you to sleep, Paige," someone nearby said.

All she could do was nod and mumble something unintelligible. And then, everything went blank.

WENDY SAT in the waiting room holding Bruce's hand. Simon, Andy, Natalie and Adam were all there as well. She'd telephoned Natalie on the way to the hospital, knowing that she and Adam would want to be there. Paige had yet to tell them of her decision to keep the baby, but now there was a greater concern. The doctors had said it was touch and go. They were hopeful she'd survive, but not confident.

Minutes passed. Everyone sat still, waiting, seemingly lost in their own thoughts. Wendy prayed silently and fervently that Paige would survive and the baby would be delivered safely. But the pastor's words from the sermon that morning rang in her head. *Will you trust Him, regardless of His answer?* Would she? Could she? Surely God wouldn't allow Paige and the baby to die. Not after she'd just recommitted her life to Him. What purpose would that serve?

My ways are higher than Yours. Trust Me.

Wendy gulped. Drew a slow breath. *God, please help me to trust You, regardless. You know my heartfelt desire is that they both be safe, but Lord, Thy will, not mine, be done.*

When the doctor appeared, Wendy's heart plummeted to her stomach. Bruce squeezed her hand. The doctor, an attractive young woman, looked shell-shocked as she approached. Her eyes were moist, her face white. She blinked. "I'm so sorry Mrs. McCarthy. Your daughter didn't survive."

Wendy's mouth fell open. Paige couldn't be dead! This wasn't happening. "No. No…" Her heart began a freefall that took her stomach with it.

Bruce slipped his arm around her shoulder and pulled her close. She wailed into his chest. Natalie sobbed loudly beside her as she rubbed Wendy's back.

Moments passed. Slowly, Wendy gained some control and looked up. "And…and the baby? Did she survive?" She swallowed hard, her heart pounding.

The doctor nodded. "Yes, she's alive."

"Is…is she okay?"

"For now. She's tiny, but we're hopeful."

Fresh tears spilled down Wendy's cheeks. "May…may we see them both?"

The doctor nodded. "Give us a few moments." Although she spoke in a professional manner, Wendy sensed it was the first time she'd lost someone like this and her heart went out to her.

She gave the doctor the weakest of smiles. "Thank you."

When the doctor turned and left, Wendy pulled a tissue

from her purse and wiped her face. How could this have happened? Only that morning, Paige had been alive and well. Now she was gone.

> *'The life of mortals is like grass,*
> *they flourish like a flower of the field;*
> *the wind blows over it and it is gone,*
> *and its place remembers it no more.*
> *But from everlasting to everlasting*
> *the Lord's love is with those who fear Him,*
> *and His righteousness with their children's children.'*

"Paige is safe in the Father's arms, my love." Bruce kissed the side of her head. "Praise God for His perfect timing."

Yes. Praise God that she gave her life to Him anew. If nothing else, they had confidence she was saved, but that didn't help with the grief and shock Wendy was feeling right now.

She looked up at Natalie. Her eyes brimmed with tears. Wendy hugged her tight. She was unable to speak.

Natalie sobbed against her shoulder. "I can't believe it."

"Neither can I." Fresh tears seeped from Wendy's eyes.

"How did it happen?" Natalie's voice wobbled.

"I don't know. I truly don't know."

"It doesn't seem right." Natalie blew her nose. "If there was something wrong, why didn't her doctor pick up something at her last check?"

"It came on suddenly. She was fine this morning."

As Natalie drew a long breath, her body shuddered. "I...I wonder if the baby will live."

An ache tore through Wendy's heart. If she lived, the tiny baby would never know her mother. She squeezed Natalie's hand. "Let's pray she does. But we have to trust God, whatever happens. He knows best."

"I know. I can't understand it, though."

"Neither can I, darling. We're certainly being tested."

The swing door opened and the doctor reappeared. "You can go in now. Immediate family members only, though."

Wendy's jaw dropped when Simon took Andy's hand and said he was family. Clarity hit her in that moment like a baseball to the head. *Her son was gay.* How had she not seen it? She tried to pretend she already knew. That it didn't bother her. She couldn't process this now. Not with her daughter just gone and a new little granddaughter struggling for life. This would have to wait. She stood, gripped Bruce's hand, and walked with him to say good-bye to Paige and to meet their new granddaughter.

Wendy could barely contain her grief as she and Bruce stood over Paige's body. Her face was pale, delicate, ethereal, and her body, still and lifeless. Why would God have allowed this to happen? Why would He have allowed her to die when she'd just returned to Him? Wendy had no answer. All she could do was trust that He had something better planned for her that they couldn't even start to imagine.

She touched Paige's pale skin lightly with her hand. "My darling girl. God bless you, sweetheart. I love you so much and I'm going to miss you like you'll never know." She swallowed the lump in her throat and bent down to kiss her, but instead, she sat on the bed and pulled Paige's lifeless body close. She rocked and kissed her as her heart ached with grief and loss.

"We'll take good care of your baby, darling. Please don't worry about her." Wendy's tears splashed onto Paige's head.

Finally, when she released Paige's body, Bruce pulled her close. She leaned against him and wept.

APPROACHING the incubator containing the tiniest baby she'd ever seen, Natalie's heart was heavy with emotion. Grief over her sister's untimely and unexpected passing mixed with relief that the baby had survived. And love. Love for this tiny gift from God. After their second failed IVF attempt, she and Adam had accepted that, other than a miracle, they would not have their own child, but they'd also sensed that Paige would decide to keep hers. Her death changed everything.

She and Adam would love this little baby as if she was their own. The doctor had told them she had every chance of survival. Although tiny, she was almost fully developed but unable to breathe on her own, and since her immune system was still developing, she was susceptible to disease. Feeding would also be a challenge, but she would make it. She'd never know her mother, and that fact grieved Natalie. It was so sad. Mum had told her that Paige had recommitted her life to the Lord the previous night, and that news filled her with joy, but that joy was now tinged with sadness.

Adam stood beside her and slipped his arm around her waist as they gazed at their little girl. "She's beautiful."

Tears welled in Natalie's eyes. "She's perfect. Just perfect."

CHAPTER 18

*F*ive days later

"'I declare to you, brothers and sisters, that flesh and blood cannot inherit the kingdom of God, nor does the perishable inherit the imperishable. Listen, I tell you a mystery: We will not all sleep, but we will all be changed—in a flash, in the twinkling of an eye, at the last trumpet. For the trumpet will sound, the dead will be raised imperishable, and we will be changed. For the perishable must clothe itself with the imperishable, and the mortal with immortality. When the perishable has been clothed with the imperishable, and the mortal with immortality, then the saying that is written will come true: 'Death has been swallowed up in victory.' Where, O death, is your victory? Where, O death, is your sting? The sting of death is sin, and the power of sin is the law. But thanks be to God! He gives us the victory through our Lord Jesus Christ.'"

"Welcome, dear friends. As we gather together to celebrate the life of our precious daughter, sister and friend, Paige

Elysha Miller, let us remember that truth. Death has been swallowed up in victory for those who love the Lord. While Paige may be absent from this earth, we have confidence that she's singing with the angels beside her beloved father."

Tears streamed down Wendy's cheeks as she imagined her precious Greg and Paige together. In many ways, Paige's prayers had been answered. Not in the way she expected or wanted, but she was now not only with God, but with Greg. Wendy doubted she could be any happier. And she could rest in the knowledge that her tiny daughter would be loved and cared for by Natalie and Adam. They'd named her Elysha Grace, a name that suited the little baby girl perfectly.

"We who are left behind will grieve. That's natural. Until we too pass from this life into the next, we're unable to comprehend the full majesty of what awaits us in heaven, but take comfort that death truly has lost its sting for those who believe, and that we need not fear death."

Wendy clutched Bruce's hand as Pastor Will McDonald continued. They'd both been touched by death. Greg, Faith, and now Paige. Death was part of life, and although she knew there was a life to come, it made her thankful for every day she had with Bruce and her two remaining children. But oh, how God needed to work in her heart to accept her son's relationship with Andy. She had no idea what He expected her to do other than love him. Andy was such a lovely young man. Finding out he was gay shouldn't have changed her attitude towards him, but somehow, she looked at them both a little differently now.

She glanced at them sitting together and had no idea what she should think, say or do. Bruce squeezed her hand. He knew what she was thinking and they'd work through it together. He'd supported her through the most trying of times, and he'd support her through this, too.

Pastor Will invited the mourners to stand and sing 'When the Roll is Called Up Yonder', Paige's favourite hymn from her youth, when she was on fire for the Lord, before Greg died and her life spiraled out of control. As Wendy sang, through her grief, she praised God once again for His truly amazing, undeserved grace that gave them hope of an eternal future and life everlasting, and that Paige's name was on the roll.

When the trumpet of the Lord shall sound,
and time shall be no more,
and the morning breaks, eternal, bright and fair;
when the saved of earth shall gather
over on the other shore,
and the roll is called up yonder, I'll be there.

When the roll is called up yonder,
when the roll is called up yonder,
when the roll is called up yonder,
when the roll is called up yonder, I'll be there.

CHAPTER 19

"Should we postpone the family coming for Christmas?" Bruce asked Wendy the night after Paige's funeral service as they prepared for bed.

"No, darling. They need to come. You need to see them. Please don't put them off."

He encircled her from behind and held her tight, nuzzling her neck. "As long as you're sure. I know you're drained."

She leaned her head against his chest and placed her hands on his. "I'll feel better after a good sleep. And besides, I'm looking forward to seeing them as well. It was almost as much of a shock to them as it was to us."

"Aiden's taking it badly. He only talked with Paige the night before she died."

"I know. And Simon's not handling it well, either. I want to have a long talk with him sometime soon, although I have no idea what I'll say. But I need to talk with him. I can't pussy-foot around him much longer."

"God will give you the words. He loves Simon just as much as you do."

"Yes, but I'm still struggling with my son being gay. Greg would have been so disappointed."

"But he still would have loved him. Just like I do."

She turned around and gazed into Bruce's eyes. "You're a good man, Bruce McCarthy. God knew what He was doing when He brought you into my life."

"And you're a good woman, Wendy, my love. God doesn't make mistakes."

"No, He doesn't."

She closed her eyes and wondered what the future held, for all of them. For little baby Elysha who was still in the hospital but was progressing well. For Natalie and Adam as new parents. For Simon and Andy, and for all of Bruce's family. But Wendy knew she needn't worry, because she knew Who held the future. She would entrust them into God's loving care, knowing He loved them even more than she.

Peace I leave with you; My peace I give you. I do not give to you as the world gives. Do not let your hearts be troubled and do not be afraid. John 14:27

A NOTE FROM THE AUTHOR

I hope you enjoyed "A Time to Care" as much as I enjoyed writing it. Wendy and Bruce's story continues in "A Time to Abide", which will be available soon! (I promise!)

To make sure you don't miss it, and to be notified of all my new releases, why not join my Readers' list. You'll also receive a free thank-you copy of "Hank and Sarah - A Love Story", a clean love story with God at the center. Go to: http://juliette-duncan.com/subscribe/

Enjoyed "A Time to Care"? You can make a big difference. Help other people find this book by writing a review and telling them why you liked it. Honest reviews of my books help bring them to the attention of other readers just like yourself, and I'd be very grateful if you could spare just five minutes to leave a review (it can be as short as you like) on the book's Amazon page.

Oh, and keep reading for a bonus chapter of "Tender Love". If you enjoyed "A Time to Care", I'm sure you'll enjoy this one too.

Blessings,
Juliette

Tender Love

Chapter 1

Brisbane, Australia

Early morning sunshine streamed through the white lace curtains of Tessa Scott's pocket-sized bedroom, but inside her heart, it rained. Nearly three months had passed since she had formally ended her relationship with Michael Urbane, and although she firmly believed it had been the right thing to do, pain still squeezed her heart whenever she thought of him.

Some days were easier than others, but the past two days had been especially hard. Yesterday had been Michael's birthday. How tempted she'd been to call him and at least wish him 'happy birthday'. Last year she'd surprised him with a day trip snorkelling on Moreton Island. They'd had so much fun—they always did, and the very memory of that wonderfully happy, sun-filled day only made it worse. She shouldn't let her mind go there, but she couldn't help it, and images of their day snorkelling amongst the coral and the myriads of brightly coloured fish played over and over in her mind.

Burying her head in her pillow, Tessa sobbed silent tears. It hurt so badly. If only the accident at his work hadn't happened. *Or he hadn't lied about the drugs.* She inhaled deeply as a sob escaped, sending another wave of sadness through her body. *Why couldn't she let go?* Maybe she should give him another chance? *But it would never be the same.* She knew that. Their adventure had died, and she needed to accept it.

A soft knock on the door interrupted her thoughts. The gentle but firm voice of her housemate, Stephanie, sounded on the other side. "Tess, you need to get up."

Tessa buried her head deeper in the pillows.

The door creaked open and Stephanie tip-toed in, placing a cup of spiced chai tea on Tessa's nightstand. The aromatic mixture of cardamom, cinnamon, ginger and other herbs filled the room, tickling her nose. Steph knew the trick to getting her up.

She gave in and raised her head. "What time is it?"

"Time to get up, that's what." Dressed in a smart business suit, Stephanie placed her hands on her hips and studied Tessa with an air of disapproval. "Don't tell me you've been crying over Michael again?"

Tessa sat up and took a sip of tea before meeting her friend's gaze. "Just thinking about him, that's all."

Stephanie shook her head and let out a frustrated sigh. "I know you're grieving, but it's been months since you broke up. Come on. Get out of bed and get ready for work. Your boss called and said she'd place you on unpaid leave if you call in sick one more time. I was tempted to tell her you weren't even sick."

"But I have been sick." Tessa leaned back against her bedhead and bit her lip, forcing herself not to cry in front of Stephanie.

"I know." Sitting on the edge of the bed, Stephanie took hold of Tessa's free hand. "It's hard to let go, especially having been together for so long. But breaking up was the only option. You know that."

"But maybe I was too hard on him." Tessa grabbed a tissue and wiped her eyes. "Those drugs changed him, Steph. He wasn't himself."

"I know. But you did try to help him. For months. I watched you slowly being torn apart. The truth is, you can't help someone who doesn't want to be helped." Stephanie squeezed her hand. "You can't help someone who lies to you about their addiction, even if it is to prescription drugs. *And he stole from you.* You need honesty in your relationship, and Michael wasn't willing to give that to you. You did the right thing. You're better off without him."

"It's just hard not knowing where he is or how he's doing." Tessa glanced at the photo of him still sitting on her dresser. "It's hard being single again. I feel ..." She paused and searched for the right word, as the ache in her chest grew. "Lonely."

"You poor thing." Stephanie leaned forward and hugged her tightly. "I'm here for you, Tess. And so's God, you know that. I understand you feel bad about this whole situation, but God's with you, and He'll help you through it. And you never know what, or who, He might have in store for you!" She gently brushed the stray hair from Tessa's face and gave her another hug.

Tessa nodded reluctantly. Steph was right. She'd made the right decision and knew that God would be with her and would help her through it, but translating that knowledge to her heart was another matter altogether.

"Come on kiddo, breakfast's ready. Let's get you up, dressed, and off to work."

Tessa slid out of bed as Stephanie retreated to the kitchen. As she swallowed down the rest of her tea, Michael's photo caught her attention once again. Grey eyes with a hint of blue in a tanned, chiselled face stared out at her, tugging at her heart-strings. She picked up the photo and flopped back onto her bed, gazing at the face that was so familiar. This torture had to end. She traced the outline of his face with her finger before hugging the photo to her chest. Closing her eyes, she squeezed back hot tears. This was it. The end.

"God, please help me get through this day." Her body shuddered as she gulped down unbidden sobs. *"I'm sorry it's taken so long, but I'm ready to let go. Please help me."* Tears streamed down her face as she hugged the photo tightly one last time before she opened the bottom drawer of her dresser and stuffed the photo under the pile of chunky knit sweaters she rarely wore.

Time to move on, and with God's help, she would.

To keep reading "Tender Love" go to

www.julietteduncan.com/library

OTHER BOOKS BY JULIETTE DUNCAN

Find all of Juliette Duncan's books on her website:
www.julietteduncan.com/library

A Time for Everything Series

A Time For Everything Series is a series of mature-age contemporary Christian romance novels set in Sydney, Australia, and Texas, USA. If you like real-life characters, faith-filled families, and friendships that become something more, then you'll love Juliette Duncan's inspirational second-chance romance.

Billionaires with Heart Christian Romance Series

Her Kind-Hearted Billionaire

A reluctant billionaire, a grieving young woman, and the trip that changes their lives forever...

Her Generous Billionaire

A grieving billionaire, a solo mother, and a woman determined to sabotage their relationship...

Her Disgraced Billionaire

A messed up billionaire who lands in jail, a nurse who throws a challenge he can't refuse...

"The Billionaires with Heart Christian Romance Series" is a series of stand-alone books that are both God honoring and entertaining. Get your copy now,

enjoy and be blessed!

The True Love Series

Set in Australia, what starts out as simple love story grows into a family saga, including a dad battling bouts of depression and guilt, an ex-wife with issues of her own, and a young step-mum trying to mother a teenager who's confused and hurting. Through it all, a love story is woven. A love story between a caring God and His precious children as He gently draws them to Himself and walks with them through the trials and joys of life.

"A beautiful Christian story. I enjoyed all of the books in this series. They all brought out Christian concepts of faith in action."

"Wonderful set of books. Weaving the books from story to story. Family living, God, & learning to trust Him with all their hearts."

The Precious Love Series

The Precious Love Series continues the story of Ben, Tessa and Jayden from the The True Love Series, although each book can be read on its own. All of the books in this series will warm your heart and draw you closer to the God who loves and cherishes you without condition.

"I loved all the books by Juliette, but those about Jaydon and Angie's stories are my favorites...can't wait for the next one..."

"Juliette Duncan has earned my highest respect as a Christian romance writer. She continues to write such touching stories about real life and the tragedies, turmoils, and joys that happen while we are living. The words that she uses to write about her characters relationships with God can only come from someone that has had a very close & special with her Lord and Savior herself. I have read all of her books and if you are a reader of Christian fiction books I would highly recommend her books." Vicki

The Shadows Series

An inspirational romance, a story of passion and love, and of God's inexplicable desire to free people from pasts that haunt them so they can live a life full of His peace, love and forgiveness, regardless of the circumstances.

Book 1, *"Lingering Shadows"* is set in England, and follows the story of Lizzy, a headstrong, impulsive young lady from a privileged background, and Daniel, a roguish Irishman who sweeps her off her feet. But can Lizzy leave the shadows of her past behind and give Daniel the love he deserves, and will Daniel find freedom and release in God?

Hank and Sarah - A Love Story, *the Prequel to "The Madeleine Richards Series" is a FREE thank you gift for joining my mailing list. You'll also be the first to hear about my next books and get exclusive sneak previews. Get your free copy at www.julietteduncan.com/subscribe*

The Madeleine Richards Series

Although the 3 book series is intended mainly for pre-teen/ Middle Grade girls, it's been read and enjoyed by people of all ages.

"Juliette has a fabulous way of bringing her characters to life. Maddy is at typical teenager with authentic views and actions that truly make it feel like you are feeling her pain and angst. You want to enter into her situation and make everything better. Mom and soon to be dad respond to her with love and gentle persuasion while maintaining their faith and trust in Jesus, whom they know, will give them wisdom as they continue on their lives journey. Appropriate for teenage readers but any age can enjoy." Amazon Reader

The Potter's House Books...stories of hope, redemption, and second chances. Find out more here:

http://pottershousebooks.com/our-books/

The Homecoming

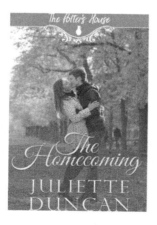

Kayla McCormack is a famous pop-star, but her life is a mess. Dane Carmichael has a disability, but he has a heart for God. He had a crush on her at school, but she doesn't remember him. His simple faith and life fascinate her, But can she surrender her life of fame and fortune to find true love?

Unchained

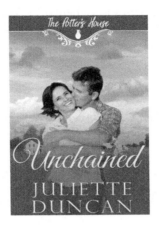

Imprisoned by greed – redeemed by love

Sally Richardson has it all. A devout, hard-working, well-respected husband, two great kids, a beautiful home, wonderful friends. Her life is perfect. Until it isn't.

When Brad Richardson, accountant, business owner, and respected church member, is sentenced to five years in jail, Sally is shell-shocked. How had she not known about her husband's fraudulent activity? And how, as an upstanding member of their tight-knit community, did he ever think he'd get away with it? He's defrauded clients, friends, and fellow church members. She doubts she can ever trust him again.

Locked up with murderers and armed robbers, Brad knows that the only way to survive his incarceration is to seek God with all his heart - something he should have done years ago. But how does he convince his family that his remorse is genuine? Will they ever forgive him?

He's failed them. But most of all, he's failed God. His poor decisions have ruined this once perfect family.

They've lost everything they once held dear. Will they lose each other as well?

Blessings of Love

She's going on mission to help others. He's going to win her heart.

Skye Matthews, bright, bubbly and a committed social work major, is the pastor's daughter. She's in love with Scott Anderson, the most eligible bachelor, not just at church, but in the entire town.

Scott lavishes her with flowers and jewellery and treats her like a lady, and Skye has no doubt that life with him would be amazing. And yet, sometimes, she can't help but feel he isn't committed enough. Not to her, but to God.

She knows how important Scott's work is to him, but she has a niggling feeling that he isn't prioritising his faith, and that concerns her. If only he'd join her on the mission trip to Burkina Faso...

Scott Anderson, a smart, handsome civil engineering graduate, has just received the promotion he's been working for for months. At age twenty-four, he's the youngest employee to ever hold a position of this calibre, and he's pumped.

Scott has been dating Skye long enough to know that she's 'the one', but just when he's about to propose, she asks him to go on mission with her. His plans of marrying her are thrown to the wind.

Can he jeopardise his career to go somewhere he's never heard of, to work amongst people he'd normally ignore?

If it's the only way to get a ring on Skye's finger, he might just risk it...

And can Skye's faith last the distance when she's confronted with a truth she never expected?

∾

Stand Alone Christian Romantic Suspense

Leave Before He Kills You

CHRISTIAN ROMANTIC SUSPENSE

LEAVE
BEFORE
HE KILLS YOU

JULIETTE DUNCAN

When his face grew angry, I knew he could murder…

That face drove me and my three young daughters to flee across Australia.

I doubted he'd ever touch the girls, but if I wanted to live and see them grow, I had to do something.

The plan my friend had proposed was daring and bold, but it also gave me hope.

My heart thumped. What if he followed?

Radical, honest and real, this Christian romantic suspense is one woman's journey to freedom you won't put down…get your copy and read it now.

ABOUT THE AUTHOR

Juliette Duncan is a Christian fiction author, passionate about writing stories that will touch her readers' hearts and make a difference in their lives. Although a trained school teacher, Juliette spent many years working alongside her husband in their own business, but is now relishing the opportunity to follow her passion for writing stories she herself would love to read. Based in Brisbane, Australia, Juliette and her husband have five adult children, seven grandchildren, and an elderly long haired dachshund. Apart from writing, Juliette loves exploring the great world we live in, and has travelled extensively, both within Australia and overseas. She also enjoys social dancing and eating out.

Connect with Juliette:

Email: juliette@julietteduncan.com

Website: www.julietteduncan.com

Facebook: www.facebook.com/JulietteDuncanAuthor

Twitter: https://twitter.com/Juliette_Duncan

Made in the USA
Middletown, DE
17 July 2021